Carnival

ON

Union Station

EarthCent Ambassador Series:

Date Night on Union Station

Alien Night on Union Station

High Priest on Union Station

Spy Night on Union Station

Carnival on Union Station

Wanderers on Union Station

Vacation on Union Station

Guest Night on Union Station

Word Night on Union Station

Party Night on Union Station

Review Night on Union Station

Family Night on Union Station

Book Night on Union Station

LARP Night on Union Station

Book Five of EarthCent Ambassador

Carnival on Union Station

Foner Books

ISBN 978-1-948691-07-9

Copyright 2015 by E. M. Foner

Northampton, Massachusetts

One

"In conclusion, it is the view of Union Station Embassy that the growing number of Gem defectors seeking refuge and employment on the station is beginning to have a deleterious effect on the local market economy, and may also portend the impending collapse of the forty-billion-strong Gem empire, forcing the other species on the tunnel network to choose sides in a messy civil war."

Kelly concluded her usual Friday afternoon report for EarthCent on this down note and leaned back in her chair. Next to the display desk, Samuel, who had long since mastered the art of pulling himself to his feet using the webbed sides of his playpen, beamed his mother a happy smile.

"Yes, Sammy. We'll be going home in a few minutes," Kelly told him. "Mommy just has to talk to Aunty Libby about the nasty clones."

"Before we talk about the Gem, is somebody aware that today is the deadline to submit a candidate hologram for the Carnival election?" Libby asked over the office speakers.

"You couldn't pay me to be the Carnival Queen," Kelly retorted. "Bork told me that the job means you have to run the complaints department in Gryph's place for a Stryx beat. Even if that's just a few hours, it sounds more like a punishment than a prize."

"A Stryx beat is a little less than two days on your human calendar," Libby informed the ambassador. "Carnival is held on the stations every ten thousand beats, roughly once every fifty Earth years."

"That's even worse, then," Kelly replied. "And I understand that the last Carnival Queen, or was it a King, had to flee the station after being accused of ignoring the rules in selecting the winner of some silly contest."

"It was a five-legged sack race, and the Dollnick ambassador in question was near the end of his term anyway," Libby replied. "I really don't know how these rumors get started."

"All the same, I'll just leave the Carnival honors to the ambassador of some species who wants it," Kelly said. "Besides, I also heard that Gryph allows cheating in the election, so it just goes to whichever species figures out how to rig the ballot."

"Does the term 'bad sport' translate properly into English?" Libby inquired sweetly.

"I'm not sure," Kelly parried. "Does 'Bah! Humbug!' work in Stryx?"

"Very well," Libby replied, affecting a sniff. "I believe you had a question about the Gem?"

"A group of Gem identifying themselves as the local underground leaders has asked to meet me, and I'm not really comfortable with the idea," Kelly explained. "I didn't mention it in my weekly report because I'm never sure about communications security anymore, but I guess the dissident Gem have viewed us as potential allies ever since the double agent stunt that Blythe ran for EarthCent

Intelligence. Why don't they approach the older and more powerful species, or talk directly with the Stryx?"

"The Gem are really something of a special case," Libby answered thoughtfully. "Gryph has been effectively granting asylum to the fugitive clones who reach the station, which he does by informing the Gem hierarchy that the nonconforming sisters are under our protection. The defectors themselves never approach us to ask for help, no doubt due to their fundamental distrust of authority. I suppose they feel safe with humans precisely because you aren't powerful."

"But humanity can't afford to offend the Gem Empire," Kelly objected. "I mean, sure, I can get away with turning down their dinner invitations, but all of the species do that."

"And you've been getting complaints about Gem dissidents taking low-paid jobs away from humans?"

"It's not exactly that," Kelly mumbled. "They're causing an imbalance between supply and demand."

"Please elaborate," the Stryx librarian prompted the ambassador.

"Well, it's how they spend their pay," Kelly griped. "You know that most of the humanoid species on the station can eat Earth fruits. The Frunge are big customers for our wine and liquor imports and the Drazens can eat anything without MSG. But as long as I've known the Gem, they've been subsisting on that awful all-in-one nutrient drink."

"Have you ever asked the Gem why they abandoned their ag deck in favor of an artificial drink produced in factories?" Libby inquired.

"I don't have to ask to know the answer," Kelly replied. "Ambassador Gem would tell me that the drink is superior to organic foods grown in unsanitary conditions, and that all of the other species are jealous of the Empire's scientific nutrition."

"Perhaps that's just the line maintained by the Gem leadership, and you'll get a different answer if you ask one of the sisters who have defected," Libby suggested. "So what exactly is the problem you're having with the way the dissident Gem, or Free Gem as they are calling themselves, have been spending their wages?"

"They're buying all of our chocolate!" Kelly exploded. "It's not just me complaining, it's all of the women I know. No sooner does a trader bring in a new shipment, the Free Gem are lined up in the Shuk and at the Chocolate Emporium in the Little Apple to grab it all. And it's not just the ready-to-eat chocolate they're buying, it's the baking ingredients too. I stopped at Hole Universe to get a triple chocolate donut yesterday, and they didn't even have the single chocolate version. I had to bribe the kid to sell me six chocolate chips wrapped in a napkin from the emergency stash he keeps under the counter. I think I'm going into withdrawal."

"My, that does sound serious," Libby responded dryly. "Should I ask Gryph to clap the refugees in irons and turn them over to the Gem military?"

"Never make fun of an addict," Kelly warned her Stryx friend. "The importers keep upping their orders from Earth, but the Free Gem are multiplying even faster. Do you know how many there are on the station?"

"Unofficially?" Libby asked. "Fewer than ten thousand dissidents at last count, though their numbers are growing at a surprising pace. Ah, you have a visitor," the station librarian cut herself off mid-discussion.

Kelly rose and stuck her head out of her office just as the outer door to the embassy slid open.

"Dring!" she cried joyfully. "Are you back for good? You have to eat dinner with us tonight, but first come in and see my baby."

"I am pleased to see you as well," the chubby little dinosaur responded cheerily. "Metoo and I have left the Kasilians to colonize their new world, and I came to see you as soon as I could. Why is your baby in a cage?"

"It's not a cage, it's a playpen," Kelly explained. "Even at home, we keep Sammy in a playpen if nobody is watching him closely."

"May I pick him up?"

"Of course. But he's never seen a Maker before, so don't be surprised if he starts crying."

Dring reached over the side of the playpen and scooped up Samuel, who clung to the little dinosaur and laughed.

"A born diplomat," Dring commented. The shape-shifter paused to take a careful inventory of the baby's parts. "He appears to be complete."

"It's polite to say something like, 'Oh, what a beautiful baby,'" Kelly hinted.

"Well, he does bear a striking resemblance to Joe," Dring hazarded a compliment. "Was that appropriate?"

"Never mind," Kelly replied with a sigh. "Wait, you said that Metoo is with you? Does that mean the Kasilians selected a new High Priest? I thought there was going to be a problem with that after Metoo solved all of their challenge questions."

"Yes, but in the end they just went back to their old method of choosing leaders," Dring replied.

"An election?" Kelly guessed.

"A ruler," Dring answered. "The tallest Kasilian became the new High Priest. I've always meant to ask you if that's where the word 'ruler' comes from in English."

"No. The two words sound the same and are spelled the same but they come from different roots," Kelly explained. "I think that makes them homophones rather than just homonyms, but I'd have to check a dictionary or ask Libby."

"I suppose it's not surprising," Dring commented, as he nuzzled the baby with his snout. "I understand that there are still some thousands of languages spoken by humans and I hope you are doing something to preserve them for the future. After a few millennia on the tunnel network, most civilizations end up with a single common tongue for the entire species. It happens surprisingly rapidly."

"Guh," Samuel said.

"Is that English, or do babies speak a different language?" Dring inquired.

"It's just baby talk, but he can say 'Mama' when he wants to. Say 'Mama' for Uncle Dring, Sammy," Kelly prompted the baby.

"Guh," Samuel responded happily.

"Speaking of Gryph, he brought us up-to-date on current events during the docking approach," Dring continued. "I'm pleased that we arrived back in time for Carnival, and I'm planning on entering the art competition if I can find an unaffiliated slot. I hope I can count on your support."

"I think you do beautiful work, Dring. You shouldn't be shy about displaying it," Kelly encouraged him.

"I'm not shy," Dring replied. "I would like to win the first prize if I enter, and if you are elected Carnival Queen, you automatically qualify for all of the judging panels and are given a double vote. It's my first opportunity to compete in Carnival and I want to make a good impression."

"But I don't want to be queen of anything," Kelly protested. "And I'm surprised you would even think about winning that way."

"We're talking about art," Dring responded in bewilderment. "It's not like a pie-eating contest or the prize for whoever grows the biggest Rinty bubble. Even within a single culture, judging art is highly subjective. Galactic art contests are really a referendum on the artist."

"One should always play fairly when one has the winning cards," Kelly quoted at Dring, knowing him to be a fan of Oscar Wilde. Just saying the line evoked a memory of how much she had missed their book discussions back when she was out on maternity leave and reread several of her old favorites. "But like I told you, I'm not running for anything. Libby just asked me to submit a hologram for the candidate promotions and I declined."

"While I've never been able to participate in a Carnival, I have studied the history and traditions," Dring told her, handing over the now squirming baby. "I believe the candidate pool is restricted to the top representative of each species with a diplomatic presence on the station. An unhappy alternative is before you, Elizabeth."

"Elizabeth?" Kelly repeated. "Oh, wait. You're quoting, wait, I'm out of practice at this, give me a second, uh, Pride and Prejudice!"

"Two points," Dring acknowledged. "But in truth, I don't think you can opt out of this."

"Libby?" Kelly asked. "Can you explain to Dring that I'm not running?"

"Welcome back, Dring," Libby greeted the Maker. "I hope that your time with the Kasilians was enjoyable, and I want to thank you in my capacity as Metoo's schoolmaster for keeping an eye on him during his reign."

"You're very welcome, Libby," Dring replied. "I know that Metoo is looking forward to returning to school and his human friends."

"Tell Dring that I'm not participating in the election campaign," Kelly interrupted impatiently, seeing nothing but pitfalls ahead if she found herself compelled to become a candidate.

"The ambassador is not participating in the election campaign," Libby confirmed. Kelly relaxed and shot Dring a triumphant look.

"Is she a candidate?" Dring asked.

"Of course," Libby replied. "Candidacy is implicit with the assumption of an ambassadorship or equivalent post on Stryx stations, and it's also spelled out in black and white in the End User License Agreement for diplomatic implants."

"Hold on a minute!" Kelly protested. "You're saying that even if I boycott the election process, I can be declared Carnival Queen against my will? Why didn't you tell me?"

"I thought you were just being modest," Libby replied. "I picked out a nice hologram from our archives to submit for you. Do you remember your speech at the ice harvesting treaty conference?"

"Oh, no," Kelly groaned, giving in to the inevitable. The details of the treaty conference were a bit hazy in her memory, but she seemed to recall crying on the podium. "Is it too late to pick my own hologram?"

"I already submitted my choice to the official Carnival committee, but if we act quickly, I suppose I could slip a new one in its place without anybody noticing," Libby answered. "Just stand up straight and I'll use the station security system to create a hologram right now."

Kelly obeyed reflexively, standing upright with Samuel cradled in her arms, looking straight ahead since she didn't have a clue where the security cameras were located. It was more likely that Libby was utilizing sensors that employed technology unimaginable to humans and could record holograms of biologicals anywhere on the station.

"Done," Libby said. "Don't be surprised when you find that your candidacy draws unified support from the humans on the station. The species of the winning ambassador gets a one-cycle rent waiver from the station manager."

"So my own constituents would have lynched me if I refused to run!" Now that she understood the consequences, Kelly didn't know if she was angry or relieved that her candidacy had become official. "If you're saying I'm the best hope for hundreds of thousands of humans to save a cycle's rent, I'll do my best, but don't expect me to spend my own money campaigning."

"Is that why you were so hesitant to step forward?" Dring asked. "Every station resident is allowed to vote for as many candidates as they choose, so elections are heavily influenced by inter-species vote-swapping pacts rather than direct campaigning."

"Well, that sounds positive, anyway," Kelly responded. She began one-handedly stuffing things she wanted to bring home for the weekend into her bag. "I'm in favor of anything that fosters cooperation among species, but didn't I also hear that it's traditionally acceptable for anybody who can figure out how to rig the ballot to do so?"

"I glanced over the statistics for the last ten thousand Carnivals on the station, and it does seem suspicious that the Verlocks win nearly a quarter of the time," Dring admitted.

"The Verlocks barely socialized with the other aliens until they started pushing that stupid game on everybody," Kelly exclaimed. "It doesn't seem likely that they would have been the best at arranging vote-swapping pacts all those years."

"No, but they are very good at math and polling algorithms," Libby commented. "Before each Carnival, the species get together to decide on a voting technology because we don't get involved in counting votes. Last time around, they settled on tamper-proof mechanical polling machines supplied by the Dollnicks. You've already missed the staging meetings for this Carnival, but I can tell you that the current Dollnick proposal was soundly rejected."

"Why didn't you warn me about this earlier?"

"I tried on several occasions, but you covered your ears and sang, 'La-la, la-la-la,'" Libby reminded her.

"Oh, right," Kelly admitted guiltily. "I was, uh, probably singing a lullaby to Samuel."

"With your ears covered?" Libby asked skeptically.

"Come on, Dring," Kelly said, deciding that retreat was in order. "Aisha always makes a vegetarian dinner on Friday, so maybe we can get you to eat something other than raw celery and carrots for a change."

Two

The ad hoc EarthCent Election Committee met in the Shuk at Baked Beans, the coffee shop favored by vendors after a long day's work. Aisha attended in place of Kelly, who used the baby as an excuse to beg off from an after-hours meeting she really didn't want to attend. The acting junior consul drafted her husband into coming along, purportedly for his deep knowledge of inter-species competitive gaming, but mainly because she was worried that everybody else would be at least twice her age.

Peter Hadad, the proprietor of Kitchen Kitsch, rose to his feet after the committee members finished their coffees and small talk. A smile twitched around the corners of his mouth as he struggled with the idea of himself as a committee chair.

"Ambassador McAllister has asked me to head this committee and I consider it an honor to serve," he began. "We've already missed most of the pre-Carnival coordination meetings with the other species, so our main task will be to encourage human participation in the various events."

"And to get the ambassador elected Carnival Queen," asserted Ian Ainsley, the current president of the Little Apple merchants group. "We all know that Gryph waived your rent for a couple of years in return for your girls helping with that auction, but speaking for the Little Apple merchants, a cycle of free rent would go a long way."

"Fair enough," Peter acknowledged. "I would also like to see the ambassador elected, but I've been doing some research with the help of the Stryx librarian, and it seems that in foregoing the pre-Carnival planning we also missed the forum in which most of the inter-species vote-swapping takes place."

"I've talked the situation over with a historian, well, with Dring, and it appears that most Carnival elections are won through voting fraud of one type or another," Paul contributed helpfully. "Given the late date, the ambassador's limited enthusiasm for campaigning, and the lack of election rules, I suggest we focus on cheating."

"Paul!" Aisha exclaimed in shock, expecting the others to join in condemnation. "These are supposed to be friendly competitions."

"Then nobody will mind a little friendly cheating," Ian observed. "But I assume we're at a severe technical disadvantage here. Some of the station species must have millions of years of practical experience in rigging elections of different sorts."

"I'm hoping to get my friend Jeeves to help," Paul answered. "The Stryx wouldn't normally be willing to interfere in something like this, but Jeeves grew up with humans and he's practically one of us. He's currently away on the auction circuit with Mr. Hadad's daughters, though, and I'm not sure he'll be back in time."

"We could raise money and buy votes," Stanley suggested. He was there in lieu of Chastity to represent InstaSitter, the biggest human employer on the station. "Where there's election fraud, there should be vote contractors willing to deliver blocks of votes for a price."

"Mr. Doogal!" Aisha remonstrated.

"I'm with the kid on this one," Ian objected immediately. "It would be too expensive. We can't hope to compete with the aliens on funds, and since the vote-sharing agreements are already in place, the aftermarket for votes from unaffiliated species will be sky-high. I'd rather invest the money in trying to hack the voting technology."

"I do have some information on that," the senior Hadad said. "The first thing I did on accepting this position was to contact the Carnival planning commission for credentials, after which I was given holo-recordings of the meetings held to date. The delegates have already narrowed the polling technology down to two proposals. The first is a statistically based extrapolation model being pushed by the Verlocks, and the second involves paying a Thark gambling consortium to handle a direct election through a special interface to their tote board for off-world betting."

"We'll have to vote for the Verlock method," Aisha said. "I don't trust anybody involved with gambling."

"Why haven't they settled on the Tharks already?" the Little Apple entrepreneur asked, taking the opposite tack. "The Verlocks are clearly too good at math to expect them to be honest with statistics."

"Unfortunately, it appears that the election planning process is as open to fraud as the election itself. The committee seems to be leaning towards the Verlock proposal, despite its obvious flaws," Peter said apologetically.

"What exactly are the Verlocks proposing?" Aisha inquired.

"They claim to have perfected a mathematical model for elections that allows them to determine the choice of a hundred million sentients based on the preferences of just three voters."

"Just three voters per species?" Aisha asked in astonishment.

"Three voters total," Peter replied, looking sadly at his empty coffee cup. "And of course, they get to pick the three. The Verlocks presented mathematical proofs for the veracity of their model and offered to give up their perpetual chairmanship of the pre-Carnival committee if anybody could find an error in the equations."

"Who gave them the perpetual chairmanship to start with?" Paul asked. "I'm beginning to see how they win so many of these elections."

"According to the official history, when the Stryx last modified the bylaws for Carnival around a half a million years ago, they thought it would be a good idea to distance themselves from the process, and let the ambassadors decide the chairmanship by a simple challenge contest," the senior Hadad replied. "Apparently, the Stryx had become frustrated with the previous methodology of electing a chairman, which required another commission to determine the election rules for the chairmanship, which required a chairman, ad infinitum."

"Committees all the way down," Stanley commented.

"Exactly," Peter confirmed. "Unfortunately, there was a Verlock in the chairman's seat when the change was made, and it's the prerogative of the seated chair to define the challenge contest. Ever since, it's been whoever can stand naked in a pool of molten rock for the longest time."

"Ouch!" Stanley winced at the thought. "Well, we won't have a chance if it comes down to three electors picked by the Verlocks, so I vote we go with the betting parlor proposal."

"Agreed," Paul and Ian concurred. Aisha sank a little lower in her chair.

14

"So we're back to the issue of recruiting humans to enter the Carnival events," Peter said. "In addition, each species is allowed to suggest one traditional event, unique to their culture, to be voted on at the same time as Carnival King or Queen."

"The same three voters?" Aisha inquired.

"Or everybody via the tote board," Peter reminded her.

"Well, I suggest caber tossing," Ian said.

"Throwing food is a sport?" Aisha asked. "I use capers in cooking sometimes, and they're too light to go very far."

"Caber, not caper." Ian seemed genuinely surprised that the others weren't up on his favorite sport. "It's an old Scottish game."

"I think I saw that in a late-night filler on one of the sports networks once," Paul said. "A pole about three times as tall as the thrower, must have weighed as much as a man too. The point was to get it to land upright or fall straight, something like that?"

"That's the ticket," Ian said. "I'm a little out of practice, I admit. I brought a caber when we originally moved here, but due to the low ceilings at the local park area, I haven't thrown since last time we visited Earth. I've been trying to organize a Highland Games on the docking deck for years."

"Where are the aliens who want to compete supposed to find a wood pole the size of a small tree on a space station?" Aisha asked.

"Now you're seeing the light, lassie," Ian replied with an exaggerated burr.

"I don't understand any of you," Aisha objected, shaking her head angrily. "Isn't the whole point of Carnival for people from different species to get together and have fun?"

"As a man who spent most of his adult life working in the gaming industry, I can assure you that all other things being equal, winning is more fun than losing," Stanley commented.

"I'm fine with caber tossing, unless you wanted to suggest traditional Hindu dancing?" Paul asked his wife.

"Me?" Aisha's eyes went wide. "No thanks. I hung up my competition slippers at sixteen. I guess we can go with the giant stick thing, but shouldn't we be consulting the other humans on the station about this?"

"Not enough time," Peter answered decisively. "The final committee vote on the election methodology is in less than twenty-four hours, and we have to submit our candidate for an elective cultural event before then. EarthCent really missed the boat on preparation for this thing for some reason. We knew in the Shuk that there was a Carnival coming, but humans just assumed that the details were all handled by the Stryx, and none of our alien friends saw fit to fill us in."

"So what do we know about the permanent events?" Stanley asked. "Are there preliminary rounds scheduled? Do contestants have to register in advance? Are we expected to put up a single human champion for each contest?"

"All good questions," the Shuk vendor responded. "The schedule for the permanent events has already been released and we have just over a month to get ready. There are no preliminary rounds. Each species is expected to present a list of contestants through its embassy, one per event. When a species can't produce a candidate for an event due to physical or mental incompatibilities, the Stryx allow that species to designate an unaffiliated sentient to fill the roster. Did I cover everything?"

"So we need to move quickly to draw up a list of humans who want to compete, and then to arrange some sort of competition of our own to pick the human champions," Stanley summed up. "I suggest we immediately post a list of the events and announce that we're holding trials starting next weekend. If we run some display ads here in the Shuk and in the Little Apple, that and word-of-mouth should do the trick."

"What are the permanent events we can compete in?" Aisha asked.

"They're primarily judged competitions, rather than contests of speed or strength," Peter answered, and consulted his notes. "Singing, two-dimensional art, three-dimensional art, four-dimensional art, cooking, beauty contest, poetry, bartering, dancing, juggling, knife throwing, clowning and best costume."

"Four-dimensional art?" Paul asked. "Is that like clocks or something?"

"No idea," Peter admitted.

"Bartering?" Ian asked.

"I suspect we'll have a lot of candidates trying out for that one," the senior Hadad replied with a smile. "Oh, and here's the fun part. All contests are judged by a panel of ambassadors who are randomly assigned to the events by the Stryx."

"Are the judges expected to cheat?" Aisha asked with trepidation, as if she were almost afraid to hear the answer.

"I'm afraid it's traditional," Hadad told her sympathetically. "The judges for each permanent event are announced in advance of the competition, which gives participants time for, er, lobbying."

"First spying, now election fraud and cheating," Aisha complained in frustration. "When I signed up for

17

EarthCent, I thought I was joining an incorruptible diplomatic mission to an enlightened galaxy. But the longer I'm here, the more it seems like Earth!"

"It's just for a week or so every fifty years," Paul told her. "Maybe the point of Carnival is to remind people what things would be like without the Stryx, but in a fun way, without the bloodshed. Kind of like your parents agreeing to let you stay up all night as a child to teach you that you need sleep."

"And there are prizes," Peter added. "It's not just a cycle of free rent for the species whose ambassador wins the election. The Stryx always give the individual winners of the competitions something to commemorate the occasion."

"Are we talking about permanent rent remission?" Ian asked hopefully.

"According to the official history, the Stryx tend to get a little creative with Carnival prizes. Nothing harmful," Peter added quickly, to reassure their potential caber tossing champion.

Three

It was Kelly's first visit to the former Gem ag deck that had been taken over by the other humanoid species when the clones halted natural food production in favor of a manufactured all-in-one nutrition drink. She had missed the fundraiser for replanting the deck and sent Aisha in her place to represent EarthCent, an event that Paul and her daughter-in-law now referred to as their first date. So when Kelly emerged from the lift tube, pushing Samuel before her in the reproduction Victorian perambulator she'd received as a baby gift from the Doogals, she didn't realize that the sparsely planted deck was a major improvement over how it had looked a year earlier.

"Not very impressive for a park, is it?" she murmured to her baby, who being sound asleep, didn't reply. There was nobody in sight near the lift tube, though a trash container full of candy bar wrappers proved that the Free Gem had been there since the last time a maintenance bot came around. Kelly thought she could hear singing coming from somewhere up the deck, where the curvature of the station obscured her view. She reviewed the cryptic note from the Free Gem on her heads-up display to make sure she was in the right place, but what jumped out at her was the station time, which appeared in the top right corner of the virtual display. It was an hour behind the time displayed on her faux-mechanical wristwatch!

"Libby?" Kelly subvoced. "Am I an hour early for my meeting or is my implant malfunctioning?"

"Have you forgotten about the daylight savings time feature on your decorative timepiece again?" the station librarian asked in response.

"Drat!" the ambassador exclaimed, snapping her fingers. "They really shouldn't have designed it so that holding in those two buttons at the same time toggles that one-hour thing on and off. I'll bet Sammy did it by mistake when I let him play with the watch while I was dressing this morning. Why did people on Earth ever invent such a weird system?"

"It was introduced during your twentieth century when artificial lighting was a substantial part of the electrical demand, though the idea was first proposed over a hundred years earlier to conserve candles," Libby explained patiently, and not for the first time. "Changing the clocks twice a year was an attempt to maximize the amount of natural light during the standard school and work hours."

"Doesn't seem right, changing time," Kelly grumbled. "If I go all the way back to the embassy now, by the time I finish explaining myself to Donna and Aisha, it will be time to turn around and return here again. Can you tell me if the Free Gem I'm supposed to be meeting are here already?"

"They are probably part of the labor party working not far from your location, perhaps a ten-minute walk," Libby told her. "Your early arrival may actually be a good thing, in case the Empire Gem have been able to penetrate the Free Gem underground."

"So I just head in the direction of the singing?" Kelly asked. "Are you sure it's the Gem laborers I hear and not some other species?"

"Affirmative," Libby replied. "Although many species, including humanity, have pledged funds to pay for remediation and replanting of this humanoid-shared park deck, actual payments have lagged, and the Dollnick construction management firm has had to keep a tight lid on labor costs. The project is currently the single largest employer of Free Gem on the station because they work for peanuts."

"So I'm going to be meeting with a whole mob of clones?" Kelly asked nervously.

"No. The humanoid-shared park deck is now a designated public space. If Gryph had charged rent, it's unlikely that the reclamation committee could have raised sufficient funds to pay for tearing up all of the cloned plantings and starting over again. Being designated a public space means that workers on the deck are employed under Stryx labor laws for biologicals, which include mandatory shifts off for rest and recuperation. The majority of Gem workers are off today."

"Then I guess I better go and face the music," Kelly punned. Fortunately, there was a trodden path in the direction she chose, and the pram wheels rolled along smoothly enough, rather than trying to bury themselves up to the axles in the dirt.

The sound of the singing gradually rose in volume until the work crew came into view. Their backs were turned to her as they moved in a straight line, sowing some kind of seed from shoulder bags. Even before she was close enough to hear the soulful music without the aid of her implant, two things jumped out at Kelly. First, none of the dozen or so clones she was approaching shared the same hair color. Second, the music sounded oddly familiar, more human than alien, as if the Free Gem were imitating a spiritual from one of the innumerable alien documentaries on human history.

"Hello, there!" Kelly called loudly when she came within hailing distance. It wouldn't do to risk startling the women by waiting until she was too close. The singing ended abruptly and the clones turned with that eerie synchronization she remembered from her dinner at the Gem embassy. After a moment of hesitation, the women all lifted a hand or waved, and one with bright green hair came forward to meet her.

"I am she who sent you the message," the Gem declared earnestly. "My sisters and I are honored that you accepted the invitation."

"Thank you for inviting me," Kelly replied diplomatically, doing her best to suppress her natural distaste for clones. "I'm curious to hear why you've contacted me specifically. I didn't realize that the Gem, the Free Gem, I mean, were interested in humanity."

The green-haired woman looked disappointed, then took a deep breath and said, "I'm afraid I could not understand you. I have been studying your English language since it was decided that we should approach the humans, but it is very difficult for me. Perhaps you could speak slower?"

"You don't have a translation implant?" Kelly asked in astonishment.

"Ah, I think I understood that time," the Gem declared in relief. "You asked about our implants. Of course, we had to have them removed when we left the Empire. All Gem implants can be monitored by the security apparatus."

"You should have told me," Kelly said slowly. "I could have brought an external voice box." The Gem shook her head in frustration, so Kelly tried again. "I can bring a machine that translates English into Gem."

"Bring, brings, bringing, brought," the Gem recited by rote in an attempt to jumpstart her memory. "Yes, I understand. Please use this machine."

"I don't have it with me today." Kelly spoke slowly, pausing between her words. "I will bring it next time we meet. Today, I will ask the Stryx to translate for you."

"No Stryx!" the woman objected violently, backing away from Kelly at the same time. The other Gem moved up closer to support their leader. "The Stryx are at the top of the power structure that includes the Gem dictatorship."

"That's not exactly true," Kelly protested, but seeing an expression of fear on the face of the Free Gem representative, she fell silent. It was obvious that the clone she was speaking to had been educated or indoctrinated with a view of the galaxy that suited the Gem elite, and Kelly doubted she could overcome that in a single meeting using a limited vocabulary. She breathed in and started over again, slowly. "Why did you want to see me?"

"Yes," the clone replied, relaxing visibly. "When we first heard that your EarthCent spy agency was willing to employ individuals from nonhuman species, we thought it was a trick. But our sisters who signed up have reported that they were treated with respect, even though they had little useful information to offer. We believe that you humans are so new in the galaxy that the other species have not had time to corrupt you."

Kelly was trying to puzzle out how to respond to this when the baby began making waking up noises, so she fished him out of the carriage and began bouncing him gently in her arms.

23

"Is that a baby that you grew inside your body?" the green-haired Gem asked her in awe.

"Yes," Kelly replied proudly. "This is my baby boy, Samuel."

"A boy?" the clone asked, her eyes going wide. She exchanged looks with her sisters, and they all crowded around Kelly, staring.

"Would you like to hold him?" Kelly asked reflexively, surprising even herself. The green-haired Gem looked even more frightened by this suggestion than she had at the mention of the Stryx, but a younger clone with a close-shaved head held out her hands.

"I will not drop him," the young woman declared confidently. "I served you dinner at the embassy once, when Military Gem attacked Propaganda Gem with the cork projectile."

"You must be Waitress Gem," Kelly declared. The ambassador felt like she had discovered an old friend among the dissidents, even though they had barely exchanged a word on the prior occasion. She gingerly handed her son over to the clone, who cradled him like an expert.

"I worked in the cloning facility crèche when I was a girl," Waitress Gem said, a faraway look coming over her face as she rocked Sammy in her arms. "But they said I was too attached to the babies and spoiled them, so they reassigned me to being a waitress."

In the silence that followed, Kelly noticed that all of the Gem had closed their eyes and were swaying along with Waitress Gem, their arms cradling imaginary babies, as if they were sharing the experience telepathically. Samuel, who at two years of age was already showing Dorothy's love of being at the center of attention, gurgled happily. Kelly found herself unwilling to interrupt, and several long minutes ticked by before the young clone opened her eyes and returned the baby.

"We trust you," Waitress Gem said simply. "Please tell us how we can live like the others."

"I don't understand," Kelly said, deeply moved by the experience, but still fundamentally puzzled about what the Free Gem wanted from her. "You want me to teach you how to live like alien species?"

"We know that we have been bred in ignorance, educated to fill our role in the Gem Empire and nothing more," the spokesclone told her. "We cannot trust the history we were taught, the media we were allowed, not even the stories passed down from who knows what source. But since fleeing the Empire, my sisters and I have watched the humans, we have worked for the humans, and we've decided that we can trust you."

"Don't be too quick to trust humans," Kelly cautioned her. "We come in all types, just like the Gem." Oops, she thought. That won't make sense in translation to a clone, even if their leader was fluent, but apparently the clone understood the gist of her meaning.

"We don't trust all humans," the leader replied. "We trust you. We want your help."

"That could be a problem," Kelly replied honestly. "You know that I am the EarthCent ambassador and my job is to protect human interests. Besides, I've never led a revolution or anything like that."

The Free Gem spokeswomen frowned in concentration, rerunning Kelly's words in her head. Finally she recited, "Revolt, revolted, revolting, revolutionary, revolution. Ah. You believe we should make a revolution!"

Before the EarthCent ambassador could correct the green-haired clone, she had relayed the message to her sisters. The women burst into a very different song than the one they had been singing earlier, drowning out Kelly's protest that she'd been misunderstood.

To arms, brave sisters
With sharp and pointy things
March always forward
All hearts beating as one
To victory or death!

"Please, don't do anything hasty," Kelly begged the clones when they completed the martial song. She later learned it was a version of the Gem anthem that dated back to their civil war, though the tune was the Free Gem's take on La Marseillaise, borrowed from the popular Grenouthian documentary about human democracy. It immediately struck her that 'hasty' was unlikely to be in the Gem's limited English vocabulary, so she tried again, forcing herself to speak slowly. "Please, don't do anything now. You must take time to think about this."

"I understand," the spokesclone replied to Kelly's relief. "We must make careful plans before we strike. One does not make a revolution by singing."

"That's not, I mean, you must think about the future," Kelly insisted. The last thing she wanted was to be the trigger for a civil war, but how could she express it? She settled on quoting Camus. "There are causes worth dying for, but none worth killing for."

"Thank you," the clone replied, causing Kelly to wonder how much of her message was understood. "We have sent messengers to the Farlings, who are known to hoard genetic samples from biologicals. For a price, they will help us reestablish the long dormant genetic lines of our species, even the males. But first we must vanquish the elites who have misguided the Gem Empire for a thousand lifetimes."

"Wait," Kelly pleaded, as she tried to formulate an unambiguous statement to salvage the situation. The EarthCent ambassador realized that she was growing afraid to say anything for fear of another defective translation, and decided that the best strategy was to buy time. "We must meet again. I'll bring the translation machine."

The spokesclone of the Free Gem leadership group communed silently with her sisters for a moment before replying.

"Agreed. We will contact you with a time after conferring with our people. Our technical experts believe this deck to be fully shielded from Gem Internal Security, but the longer you are here, the greater the risk you might be discovered. Please accept a small token of our appreciation which we have prepared for you."

Kelly grimaced as she tried to figure out how to explain that as the EarthCent ambassador, she would be endangering her neutrality if she accepted a gift from the revolutionaries. Before she could finish arranging an easy-to-understand version in her head, the youngest clone of the group stepped forward and presented the ambassador with a gift bag from the Chocolate Emporium. On second thought, Kelly decided that the risk of offending the Free Gem by rejecting a heart-felt present outweighed the other political and ethical considerations.

"Thank you," she said, accepting the bag. It took all of her willpower not to look inside until she and Samuel were alone in the lift tube. Before returning to the embassy with its staff of chocoholics, she removed a bar of her favorite dark chocolate and stashed it under her son's blanket.

Four

"Joe!" Kelly cried, pointing towards the open door of the ice harvester and simultaneously knocking Paul's coffee into his lap. "I think somebody just threw a knife at us!"

Paul leapt to his feet and tried to pull off his pants even as he started for the door, resulting in a spectacular sprawl. Joe was slower out of his chair, but he was the closest one to the ramp when another knife arced by the opening and disappeared. This time it was followed by a second, and a third, and a fourth, and a fifth, until it seemed like there was a continuous arc of cutlery in the air. The ex-mercenary pulled up short and broke into a grin.

"Whatever they're doing with those knives, they aren't throwing them at us," Joe said with a laugh. "I suspect we have an overeager contestant on our hands here."

"But the tryouts aren't supposed to start for another forty-five minutes," Kelly pointed out. "Sorry about the coffee, Paul."

The embarrassed young man was back on his feet by this point, though he had decided that discretion was the better part of valor and carefully stepped out of his pants, rather than risking a burn. There was a light red patch on his upper legs where the coffee had soaked through the fabric, so he wadded them up and stalked off in the direction of the laundry room.

"Hey, get those knives away from the ship. I've got kids up here," Joe called out the door good-naturedly.

"My apologies," a woman's voice called back. "I haven't been in a space with such a high ceiling in so long that I just got carried away."

"Tell her to keep her pants on for another forty-five minutes," Kelly instructed Joe, and then both of them broke out laughing at the unintentional joke.

"I don't think that's funny at all," Aisha objected stoutly, coming to the defense of her husband. She rose and approached the opening. "You're early, the tryouts start at 8:00 AM," she called from a safe distance.

"Sorry again," the voice replied. "I'll just be practicing." The glittering pattern of knives moved slowly away from the door, and Joe and Aisha returned to the breakfast table.

"I wish Beowulf was still here," Dorothy said. "He would have told us somebody was coming."

"Beowulf has gone to the Happy Hunting Grounds," Kelly comforted her daughter. "I'll bet he's looking down right now and laughing at us."

"More likely he's laughing at Paul," Joe observed.

"Beowulf is probably a puppy back on whatever world Huravian hounds come from," Aisha told her young sister-in-law, choosing to ignore the second quip at her husband's expense.

"Is that true?" Dorothy asked, looking from Aisha to her mother. "I want him to come back, but I don't want to make him leave the Happy Hunting Grounds." Her brows furrowed in concentration and she declared, "It's a real problem."

"According to the mercenary who brought him into our group, Huravian hounds do reincarnate. But Beowulf was a genetically-engineered cross with an Earth mastiff, so I'm not sure which afterlife rule applies," Joe mused.

"If he did come back as a puppy, how will he find us?" Dorothy asked urgently. "Do dogs have money to buy space tickets?"

"Dogs have a super sense of smell," Joe reassured her. "And Beowulf is a galaxy-class mooch. I'm sure he could hitch a ride with somebody."

"If Beowulf has come back from the Happy Hunting Grounds, he's probably making some other little girl happy right now," Kelly told her daughter. She was beginning to wish the adults had taken the time to get all of their stories straight when Beowulf had passed on.

"I'm going to ask Dring," the ten-year-old decided. Since his return, the friendly shape-shifter and frequent guest had replaced Blythe as the ultimate authority on grown-up stuff in Dorothy's world.

"Finish your breakfast first," Joe instructed his daughter. He knew from experience that once her mind was made up to do something, she tended to drop everything else to pursue her goal.

"Where's Metoo?" Paul asked, coming back into the room in a new pair of pants. "This is the first day all week he's not here for breakfast."

"It's Saturday," Dorothy explained, in a tone that let Paul know he was a very silly person for having to ask. "We don't have school today. But I told him to come see the Carnival people. He's never been to one before."

"Neither have I," Jeeves announced, floating through the door. "Are you people aware that there's a young woman out there throwing knives at innocent Stryx as they float by?"

"Don't let her hit Metoo!" Dorothy ordered the robot.

"I won't," Jeeves reassured her. "I suggested she move away from the direct path between the entrance to Mac's Bones and your home."

"When did you get back from the auction circuit?" Paul asked his friend.

"Late last night, I didn't want to wake you," Jeeves replied. "I have a message for Joe, actually. I ran into your old commander, Pyun Woojin, on Echo Station. We auctioned off some antique firearms for him at a very good price. He's retired from the mercenaries and seemed to be at loose ends, so I suggested you might have work for him. It turned out he was heading this way already and he'll be dropping by sometime in the next couple days."

"What kind of job could you have for an ex-mercenary officer?" Aisha asked Joe.

Everybody at the table looked strangely at the acting junior consul, including her husband, before Dorothy took pity on her and explained. "You know. As a S - P - Y."

"Oh, right," Aisha mumbled. No matter how many times it had been spelled out for her, even with a camp full of trainees in Mac's Bones three weeks out of four, she just couldn't quite make the existence of EarthCent Intelligence part of her thought process. Her willful ignorance had gone from cute to embarrassing, especially since Blythe and Clive had rapidly grown the intelligence agency to the point that its office location was better known than the embassy's.

"So, are the two of you going to be screening the contestants yourselves, or will the other committee members help you?" Kelly asked.

"All five of us are supposed to be here, that way we won't have any ties if we have to vote," Paul said. "I don't have a clue how many candidates are going to show up, but we plastered the Shuk and the Little Apple with display ads, and then Stanley got InstaSitter to pay for some notification postings on the corridor displays. If any of the humans on the station haven't heard about Carnival yet, they must be in stasis."

"Which brings me to the second reason for my visit," Jeeves said. "Gryph and Libby have explained that it wouldn't be fair for me to interfere in the election on the ambassador's behalf. I'm sorry, Kelly."

"You're forgiven," Kelly declared, unable to hide her relief. Libby had been as good as her word and warned off her offspring from rigging the election in EarthCent's favor.

"Was it because of the rent remission thing?" Paul asked. "Could you get Kelly elected queen and then have Gryph give the cycle of free rent to the runner up?"

"I suggested that myself," Jeeves admitted. "From the point of view of the elder Stryx, the cycle of free rent is just something to get everybody involved in the elections. How's your election campaign going otherwise?"

"You were the campaign," Paul informed Jeeves sourly.

"I, for one, am glad you aren't going to interfere, Jeeves," Aisha told her husband's friend. "I really worry that everybody is missing what's important here."

"Winning?" Jeeves asked.

Aisha moaned in exaggerated fashion and buried her head in her arms, getting milk from her breakfast cereal on her nose in the process.

"This is shaping up to be a good day," Kelly said cheerfully. "After I feed Sammy, I intend to get a front row seat at the tryouts, right on my own patio."

The murmur of voices and snatches of voice exercises and lip rolls was getting harder to ignore, as early arrivals to the trials greeted each other and launched into their pre-contest intimidation routines.

"I better head out and start taking down names so we don't get jammed up," Paul said. He filched Aisha's personal tab from the table as he rose. "Are you going to hang out and watch the trials, Jeeves?"

"Perhaps later," the Stryx replied. "I understand that Dring is back on the station and I want to discuss a few things with him."

"I'll be out in a second, Paul," Joe said as the family breakfast began breaking up. "Are you coming, princess?"

"I'm going with Uncle Jeeves to see Uncle Dring," Dorothy replied, hastily finishing off her juice. "When Metoo gets here, tell him where we are."

"Right," Joe answered. He went around the table to kiss Kelly on top of the head, and then trooped down the ramp after Paul.

"Just your name and the event you're trying out for!" Paul was shouting to make himself heard over the background noise of the rapidly growing crowd. "You don't have to push for a place in line. We're not going to run off before everybody gets their chance."

"That's only because we live here," Joe commented in an undertone, surveying the small mob. He didn't want to interrupt Paul, who was repeating each registrant's information to Aisha's tab for recording, but the group didn't look particularly promising. Maybe that's why they showed up early, he thought to himself. It's the only way they can hope to be noticed.

"Hey, Joe," somebody called out from off to his side. Joe turned to see Stanley approaching. "Not a bad turnout for starters. Are the other judges here yet?"

"Uh, that's Hadad from the Shuk and somebody from the Little Apple?" Joe asked uncertainly.

"Never mind. Here's Peter now," Stanley said, as a gap suddenly appeared in the press of contestants and the senior Hadad walked through. "And the top of that ship's mast bobbing in our direction must mean that Ian's here."

"Hello, Joe. Stanley," the Shuk vendor greeted them. "Next time you're stuck in a crowd, try saying, 'I'm one of the judges.' I felt like Moses parting the Red Sea."

"Morning," Joe replied, but his eyes were on the tall shaft of wood that swayed back and forth rather alarmingly as it approached. It was upside-down for a mast, with the wider circumference at the top. Suddenly, it leaned too far to one side for the bearer to bring it back to the vertical, and it fell to the deck with an audible crash. "I hope nobody was standing under that."

A minute later, the mob gapped open again, and a red-faced, sweaty judge appeared.

"I forgot it was so heavy," Ian said, still panting for breath. "I got it upright against the bulkhead and thought I'd carry it over for practice, but I'm beginning to regret the whole thing."

"Was that a caber?" Joe asked in surprise. "How did you fit it in the lift tube capsule?"

"Corner-to-corner," the Scotsman replied proudly. "Checked the measurements with the station librarian before I came, of course. I put it down away from the crowd there, sorry about the dent. I didn't want to risk some fool getting too close while I was practicing my run-up." He broke off suddenly. "Hey, you recognized a caber!"

"Clan MacAlister," Joe replied with a crooked smile. "But we spell it like the English and I don't wear skirts."

"Maybe you can toss against me for the trial," Ian suggested eagerly. "You're a big man, and I wouldn't want everybody thinking I put the event in for myself. Just takes a little practice to get accustomed to the balance."

"Caber toss is a long way from becoming an official event," Hadad reminded him. "There's less than a month left before the election, and only five of the elective events on the ballot will be included in Carnival."

"How are we ever going to choose from so many people?" Aisha asked, emerging from the converted ice harvester to join the other committee members. "And we're supposed to see all of these contestants perform this weekend?"

"Don't worry," the committee chair reassured her. "Most, if not all of these people, are here on a lark. We'll only need a couple of minutes to sift them out. It's only in the final rounds that it'll get difficult."

"And we don't have a choice," Stanley added. "That's the way it is with all competitive events. Deadlines and rules."

"Paul seems to be working through the line pretty quick," Aisha commented. Her husband had the whole process down to asking, 'Name and Event?' and if anybody tried to engage him in conversation, he turned to the next person and continued.

"He's had plenty of tournament experience," Stanley reminded her, surveying the crowd with a practiced eye. "I'll bet there are just over two hundred people here, and the newcomers are slowing to a trickle. Shall we get started?"

"Got a stepladder I can borrow, Joe?" Peter asked.

"One stepladder coming up," Joe replied. As he strolled around the back of the ice harvester to retrieve the small aluminum ladder, it reminded him of how he used to send Beowulf for parts and tools. He missed the giant hound more than he let on, but he was resisting Kelly's suggestion to adopt a replacement.

By the time Joe returned with the ladder, it was just after 8:00 AM and Paul had already finished logging all of the applicants. It turned out that everybody had arrived early, one of the advantages to living on a space station with smart lift tubes that could always figure out where you were trying to go. Hadad, who was no taller than his daughters, climbed up a couple of steps before he started talking.

"Welcome to the first day of the trials to represent humanity in the coming Carnival," Peter began, in a penetrating voice that left no doubt as to where Shaina and Brinda had learned their trade. "I am Peter Hadad from Kitchen Kitsch on the Shuk deck, and I was appointed by Ambassador McAllister to head the EarthCent Carnival Committee. I'm sure you're all aware that this is a last-minute endeavor on our part. This is the first Carnival to take place since humans took up residence on the station and nobody was aware of the requirements."

"Why not?" called a clown from the crowd. He had an immense ball of orange hair that nearly doubled his height, and he punctuated his question by squeezing the black rubber bladder on a tin horn that made a noise like an old-fashioned cartoon. "It's why we pay taxes to EarthCent!"

"Nobody pays taxes to EarthCent," Hadad called back.

"I know, it's part of my shtick. Witty banter, get it?" the clown replied. "It's not just about running around in floppy shoes and honking the horn, you know." He added a honk for emphasis.

36

"Hey, wait your turn," a woman with a bulbous white nose cried in response. Then she turned a standing somersault and gave a triumphant honk on her own horn.

"Please people, we have a lot of auditions to go through today. What's the number, Paul?"

"Two-oh-nine," Paul replied. "That includes eleven clowns, by the way."

"How many caber throwers?" Ian asked behind his hand.

Paul pointed back at Ian in response.

"We're going to start by dividing you up into five groups, and we'll see if you can reach a consensus amongst yourselves on who should represent the human community before we start judging," Peter continued. "That's five groups so there can be a committee member with each group to try to move things along. How do the numbers work out for groups, Paul?"

"Let's put the artists together in one group, that will be the biggest. Beauty contestants, best costume and clowns will be the second biggest. Cooking, knife-throwing, tumbling and juggling will be third. Singing, poetry and dancing fourth, and barter can be its own group."

"Alright," Hadad called down from the ladder. "Everybody got that? Barter stays here with me. Singing, dancing and poetry, please follow the acting junior consul, Aisha McAllister. Aisha, take them over near the entrance. Beauty contestants, best costume and clowns are with Stanley. Sorry, Stan. Cooking, knife-throwing, tumbling and juggling with Mr. Ainsley, who runs Pub Haggis in the Little Apple. And that leaves the artists with young McAllister. Good luck, Paul. Let's all take an hour and see if we can at least settle on the top prospects before going to formal auditions."

The assembled humans didn't sound happy, but they separated into groups and followed their respective committee member to different areas of Mac's Bones to begin the winnowing process.

By the time Kelly came outside with Samuel, the only people near the ice harvester were the bickering group of barterers.

"I say that independent traders are the most qualified," insisted a man dressed in a hooded cloak that Kelly would have associated with a fairytale wizard. "We have the most experience bartering with aliens under difficult circumstances."

"But you're used to having unique goods, and customers who can't comparison shop," protested a gadget vendor from the Shuk. "I'm surrounded by competition shouting out a lower price all day long, so everybody I barter with already knows where to start."

"That's exactly why neither of you are qualified," objected a gaudily dressed woman. "You're both used to bartering your own merchandise, so you always know the secret half of the equation. I always buy with cash, so I'm used to being at a disadvantage."

"Isn't buying with cash haggling rather than bartering?" Kelly interrupted.

"Thank you, Mrs. Ambassador," Peter said. "Judgment has been rendered. Anybody whose experience is based on cash purchases is now disqualified from the bartering auditions."

There was a collective groan, and a number of nasty looks thrown in Kelly's direction, but over half of the group began packing up their things and moving to the exit. Hadad waited for them all to get underway before continuing.

"Now look," he told the remaining people. "Some of you I've bartered with in the course of business, others I know by sight. I've told the rest of you about my own background, and after thirty years in the business, I think I know a great barter-hand when I meet one. I'm betting on Mr. Clavitts, so let's give him a few minutes to talk about his experiences, and then if any of you want to challenge him, we'll work out a contest. Mr. Clavitts?"

A nondescript man in shabby coveralls and a flat cap separated himself from the group and turned to face them, like a reluctant student summoned to the front of the class to make a presentation. He looked embarrassed over being chosen as the stalking horse, and immediately set about trying to ease the mood of his rivals.

"Look here," Clavitts said. "It doesn't seem fair that Mr. Hadad is giving me the pole position in these trials based on his instincts, so I'm willing to compensate you all for hearing me out. Say, coffees all around?"

A dozen would-be champion barterers grumbled, one or two adding something about cream and sugar, but it was just about that time of the morning on the human clock, and his offer had struck a nerve.

"Alright then, let's talk about coffee shops," he continued. "Myself, I've always been a big fan of the home-brewed taste because it reminds me of the many ceremonial cups I've shared with elders on various outposts after a long day of trading. But maybe some of you prefer those new-fangled coffee drinks they make in the Little Apple."

"I prefer mine today rather than talking about it," grumbled the gadget vendor from the Shuk who had spoken earlier.

"Exactly," Clavitts replied. "So rather than sending out and waiting around, perhaps I can persuade the lovely lady with the beautiful baby to allow me access to their novel home so I can brew all of you a cup."

"Who, me?" Kelly asked in surprise, having been on the verge of strolling off to see how Aisha was doing with her group.

"I don't see any other beautiful babies here," Clavitts responded. "But if you don't have a large enough coffee urn, I'm sorry to have bothered you."

"We have all sorts of coffee makers," Kelly replied without thinking. "We're used to hosting large groups. But the house is in a bit of a mess, so perhaps you better let me brew the coffee."

"Well, now I feel bad that I even brought it up," Clavitts said apologetically. "I insist that you let me compensate you for your trouble, doesn't everybody agree?"

Peter watched in amusement as the remaining candidates joined in backing up their rival, who rooted around the pockets of his coveralls and came up with a programmable Stryx cred.

"Here," Clavitts said, extending it towards Kelly. "Please debit it for, shall we say, fifty creds, and I won't feel so bad about interrupting your morning."

"I don't have a mini-register," Kelly protested, pushing the coin away. "Besides, it's my pleasure. Now that I think of it, we should really put out refreshments for all of the candidates."

"Isn't she a good sport?" Clavitts asked, turning back to the group. "I don't know about the rest of you, but I think the least we can do is take up a collection." He removed his flat cap and tossed it to the cloaked trader. The man caught it grudgingly, dug in his pocket for some loose creds, dropped them in the cap and passed it along.

"Please, don't worry about the money," Kelly protested, but the hat was quickly making the rounds, getting heavier and producing more clinks as it went.

"Wait a minute," said the surly gadget vendor when the hat returned to Clavitts. "I see what's going on here, but this is salesmanship, not bartering."

"Life is long and full of salesmanship," Kelly offered helpfully, though she wasn't sure if it was from a book or an old movie. She'd gotten back into the habit of swapping quotes with Dring after his long absence, and now she was finding it hard to keep them out of her everyday conversations.

"Thank you, Kelly," Peter said. "Did the rest of you think that bartering is just a matter of trading items back and forth until somebody runs out? Of course it involves salesmanship, and I believe that present company included, Mr. Clavitts represents our best chance. Are there really any objections?"

A few of the bartering candidates grumbled under their breath, but nobody else was holding a hat full of money.

Five

"Welcome to Union Station, Wooj." Joe greeted his old commander as the man stepped through the arrivals gate. "Traveling light, I see."

"Hey, Joe. Your robot pal and a couple young ladies sold all of my baggage for me a few weeks back," Woojin replied readily. "When I realized it was time to call it quits, I decided that living with a collection of antique weapons wasn't going to help me move on. Got a better price than I expected, and now I'm on the market for a ship."

"I have some people you might want to talk to before you make that decision," Joe said. "Not to be pushy, but if you're feeling hungry, we could go meet them right now. I'm stag tonight because Kelly is at some sort of election committee meeting, and she took the kids along as an excuse to leave early."

"Free food sounds fine by me," Woojin replied with a laugh, and he fell in comfortably next to Joe as they started for the nearest lift tube. "Funny, the things about civilian life that take you by surprise. I still haven't gotten used to the fact that I'm expected to pay for three meals a day. And what's your wife running for this time? I thought that Ambassador was pretty much the top job slot these days."

"Carnival Queen," Joe explained, not bothering to hide his amusement with Kelly's candidacy. "She doesn't want the job but it's not really her call, came with the territory. Burgers and beers work for you?"

"Menu's fine, but I hope the choice doesn't reflect the budget of the outfit trying to recruit me."

"Naw, money's no problem. I just pinged them to say we're on our way. The menu is because we're mainly vegetarian at home these days, since Paul's wife does most of the cooking. I still flip burgers for a picnic, but other than that, I have to fit them in when I can."

"So the kid is married." Woojin shook his head in mock disbelief. "You ever think about how your life might have been different if you had never heard a mercenary recruitment pitch?"

"My wife doesn't let me," Joe replied as they stepped into the lift tube. "Burger Bar."

The lift began its run from the docking deck on the inner core up to the Little Apple, and Woojin let his rucksack slip to the floor. A couple of years younger than Joe, he was one of the last officers to graduate the national military college of the old South Korean Republic back on Earth, and he was too disciplined a soldier to let his curiosity about the dinner meeting show. Instead, he asked about Joe's children, and the proud father carried the conversation until they exited the lift tube and made their way to the pub.

"Are you starting up a new mercenary outfit?" Woojin asked Clive, after one glance at the head of EarthCent Intelligence. "No offense, but I'm through with fighting for a paycheck, and I don't want to accept your food under false pretenses."

"Nothing like that," Clive responded, and introduced himself. "We've got one more coming, but I ordered a pitcher when I got here so we should have—ope, here it comes now."

The waitress placed the tray with a pitcher of beer and four pilsner glasses on their table. She made a show of using her index finger to count the glasses and then counted the men. "Would you like to order now, or will you wait for your fourth?"

"I'm here," Lynx announced. Immediately on arrival, she pulled over one of the tall stools and clambered up. "I'll have a burger and fries, medium. And I'm Lynx Edgehouse," she added, extending a hand to Woojin.

"Pyun Woojin. Burger and fries, rare on the burger."

The waitress looked at Joe, who simply nodded. He had been ordering the same thing for the last ten years. Clive showed his independent streak by ordering a chef's salad with steak tips, the fries on the side. Joe expertly emptied the pitcher into the four glasses and offered the toast.

"To somewhere else."

"What kind of toast is that?" Lynx demanded, after the three men clicked their glasses and tilted back their beers.

"Traditional mercenary," Woojin explained concisely.

"Oh," Lynx acknowledged, and belatedly raised her glass. "Somewhere else!"

"Every time I accompany Kelly to an alien embassy for dinner, they tell us to eat first and talk business afterwards," Joe said. "But I've always found it easier to relax and eat after the business is done. Woojin here catches on as quick as anybody you're likely to meet this side of humanity, so I'll just clue him in if nobody minds."

"No objections here," Clive said. Lynx and Woojin looked at each other and shrugged, and Joe continued.

"Clive here is the head of the new EarthCent Intelligence service, and Lynx, in addition to being one of their

44

first agents, is third in the pecking order, along with filling in as EarthCent's cultural attaché on Union Station," Joe said bluntly. "We're running a casual training camp for spies in Mac's Bones, my old junkyard hold, and I'm working part-time as an instructor."

"You got a holo presentation to go along with this?" Woojin asked in jest. Nobody took the bait. "Alright, I've heard some things about your new agency and I gather secrecy isn't one of your strong points. Where do you see me fitting in?"

"It's going to sound a little funny, but we've been ignoring military skills in our agent recruitment so far," Clive said. "Most of our hires are back office analysts or amateur alien anthropologists who we're supplying to the stations as cultural attachés. We're teaching them all a little tradecraft so they'll know what to do and who to call if something important comes up, but a lot of our work has really been extending the EarthCent infrastructure beyond what the Stryx were willing to fund."

"And you want to militarize the agency?" Woojin asked skeptically.

"Not the agency, just a contingency team," Clive explained. "We haven't even decided whether we want snake-eaters on staff or just somebody who can hire them as needed. I don't have the time, Joe doesn't have the inclination, and nobody else has the experience."

"And when it comes to contingency planning, neither of us are at your level in any case," Joe added.

Woojin sipped his beer and looked towards the kitchen. "Can I think about it for a few days, or is this one of those take-it-or-leave-it deals?"

"You can have a whole month if you want," Clive replied. "We don't have any fires that need putting out, at least not that we're aware of. It's just something we'd been talking about, and then you became available."

"It's the first job I ever had with benefits," Lynx chipped in. "Come to think of it, it's the first job I ever heard of with benefits."

"You mean like, retirement?" Woojin asked incredulously. Lynx nodded, causing the middle-aged soldier to nudge Joe and grin like a boy. "Did you hear that, Joe? And you can vouch for these people's finances?"

"As long as there's a need for babysitters," his friend responded cryptically.

"Actually, the retirement fund is managed by the Stryx," Lynx told them. "I asked once, and they put it all into station real estate, which has been the safest investment in the galaxy for the last fifty or sixty million years."

"Two rare, one medium, and one chef's salad with steak tips," the waitress announced, smoothly moving plates from the floating tray onto their table. "I put all the fries in one basket to save room, so just give me a shout if you run low. Should I refill this?" she asked, taking the empty pitcher

"Yes, thank you," Joe responded. Those were the last intelligible words any of them uttered for a few minutes while the food disappeared.

"Didn't realize I was that hungry," Woojin said, breaking the conversational drought. "It's too bad your wife had the election thing tonight, Joe. I'm looking forward to meeting her."

"You'll see her in a couple of hours," Joe told him. "You're staying with us, of course."

"I appreciate that, Joe, but I already have a hotel reservation. I've always wanted to try a fancy resort, and I won a voucher for Club Asia on Union Station in the passenger

46

lottery, on the trip to Echo Station to auction off my gun collection. You must have seen their ads, right?"

"Why settle for five stars when you can have nine tails?" Lynx recited the tagline from the luxury hotel chain ad. "What does that even mean?"

"The nine-tailed fox is an important spirit in the Eastern cultures from back on Earth," Woojin explained. "In Korea, it's Gumiho, in Japan, the Kitsune, in China the Huli jing. The Gumiho is a shape-shifter that often transforms into a beautiful woman to seduce young men so it can eat their livers or their hearts."

"And getting eviscerated is your idea of a luxury vacation?" Lynx followed up.

"We all have to go sometime, it's just a question of how," the ex-mercenary replied complacently. "So, are the three of you the brain trust for this organization?"

"Uh, actually my wife sort of manages things from behind the scenes," Clive readily admitted. "She couldn't be here this evening because she's working on getting Joe's wife elected for the Carnival thing."

"I see there's no shortage of action in EarthCent Intelligence," Woojin commented. "Are you going to need me to sabotage some floats or assassinate a beauty queen?"

Lynx laughed and snorted at the same time, a mistake while trying to swallow beer, which subsequently came out of her nose.

"I guess we can't compete with the excitement of working as a caravan guard," Joe countered, pouring another round from the refilled pitcher.

"Low blow," Woojin responded. "Besides, that consortium work has been drying up as the new trade routes become established. Amazing what a game can do for interspecies relations. One of the reasons I left last month

47

was I couldn't face another one of those idiotic Vergallian wars of succession. I'm too old to lead a cavalry charge on a tech-ban world."

"I'm going to guess you're interested enough for us to move on to the next bit," Clive said. He unlatched a heavy metal bracelet from his wrist, pushed on a combination of metal studs, and laid it on the table. "Drazen tech. It will make the conversation reasonably private."

"Reasonably?" Woojin asked.

"I assume that the Drazens can listen in if they want to, it only makes sense. But they're our allies, and what I'm going to tell you about now is more sensitive than secret."

"Our Gem problem?" Lynx guessed. "Oops, sorry. I keep forgetting that it's not a test."

"I don't know if you've had any dealings with the Gem in your career, Woojin, but we're told they've been one of the more stable species on the station network since they joined after, uh, consolidating their gene pool to one individual through civil war," Clive said. "For some reason we don't understand, Gem looks to be heading into another civil war, this time against themselves, or rather, herself. The Gem dissidents, the Free Gem, are highly distrustful of everybody who is part of the galactic status-quo, which they understandably believe has ignored, if not actively supported, the rule of the Gem elite."

"Came up against them in one of my early outings," Woojin replied, searching his memory for details. "Can't say it's anything I'm proud of, basically a raid on one of their mining outposts for rare minerals. I'm not even sure who was paying us, though the rumor was that they were a group of artificials from one of the manufacturing orbitals. Outpost was well outside of Stryx space, of course, so none of the normal rules applied."

"What happened?" Lynx asked.

"We finessed the ground part of the operation. They probably thought nobody knew about the mines because they were pretty new and the star system didn't have any planets with breathable atmospheres. We hit the ground in armored spacesuits and the mine workers didn't try to argue, but by the time we loaded up the shuttles and got back into space, there were some Gem fleet elements already closing on our transport."

"Your transport a raider or a capital ship?" Clive asked.

"Old Horten cruiser. The crew who subcontracted us for the ground work must have stolen it out of a mothball orbit or bought it military surplus," Woojin continued. "Ship was already old when humans looked up at the stars and thought they were revolving around the Earth on a big glass shell. And it didn't have much for modern weaponry either, just some basic rail guns and high-energy beam weapons which were so integrated into the hull that you couldn't pull them out without turning the ship into scrap."

"Did your captain employ discretion?" Joe asked, using the mercenary code word for running away.

"No, he didn't even change colors," Woojin replied, chuckling at the thought. "Captain and crew were mainly renegade Horten, and do I ever miss playing poker with those boys. We were outnumbered three to one, though two of the Gem ships were smaller, maybe light cruiser class, but the Hortens kept banging away at them for a good hour until we were far enough out of the planet's gravity well to jump. I don't know if the Gem caught up with the ship at some later date or went after our employers. Maybe they figured there had already been enough shooting to satisfy their honor."

"I don't get it," Lynx said. "The Gem ships were regular navy and they couldn't inflict serious damage on an outdated Horten cruiser? I though those species were more or less tech-equivalent."

"Ten thousand years ago, maybe," Woojin replied. "Might also be that the Gem who engaged us were given obsolete units and relegated to patrolling low-value outposts, I don't know. But the Horten captain claimed that the Gem navy was stagnant, that they hadn't kept up with equiv-tech species for a long time, and that they weren't buyers on the open market."

"That matches what I've been hearing lately," Clive observed. "For thousands of years the Gem have been pouring all of their resources into cloning more Gem, but they don't seem to be advancing otherwise. In fact, our analysts suggest that they are actually moving backwards in some areas, like abandoning fresh food for a manufactured substitute. Although they're on the tunnel network, they're practically invisible in the galactic economy."

"But you didn't invite me here to see if I had any stories about the Gem floating around in my memory," Woojin reminded them. He poured himself about a third of a glass, which finished the second pitcher. Joe signaled to the waitress.

"There are about forty billion Gem spread around the galaxy, mainly in large clumps since they keep to themselves," Clive continued. "We know that increasing numbers have been fleeing the Gem Empire, despite the internal security apparatus, and some are trying to form an organized resistance. Although most humans have a visceral dislike for the clones, the Free Gem view us as potential allies."

"They look up to my wife for some reason," Joe added.

"So you're worried that humans will get mixed up in a Gem civil war and then become targets?" Woojin asked.

"The Stryx won't let any war spread onto the tunnel network, of course, but there are plenty of isolated human communities on farming and mining colonies, some of them well outside of Stryx space," Lynx pointed out. "If the Gem military gets nasty, especially if it looks like things are going against them, they might try for revenge."

"The Empire Gem I've met with Kelly at diplomatic events seem to take everything personally," Joe added. "Inferiority complex you could ride a horse through."

"So you're mainly thinking about contingency planning, maybe getting an early warning system in place, making sure that the isolated humans know what's going on." Woojin took the silence to be assent and drummed his fingers on the table. "I'm still going to spend the night in Club Asia," he said finally. "I'll come around and visit tomorrow when the kids are awake, Joe."

"Does that mean you took the job?" Lynx asked.

"Until I quit or you fire me," Woojin replied. "I guess I can put off exploring the galaxy on my own for a while. It probably wouldn't have been that interesting anyway."

"It's mainly exercise machines in Zero-G and eating out of squeeze tubes," Lynx concurred. "And no beer."

Six

"What are they doing?" Metoo asked Dorothy. The girl and the young Stryx were crossing Mac's Bones to visit Dring, but on the way to the disguised passage through the scrap pile, they paused for a moment to watch Joe working with a new class of EarthCent Intelligence recruits.

"Daddy says it's drilling, but they never actually make holes in anything," Dorothy explained. "They mainly shout and run in small circles. They don't bump into each other so much after the first week."

"Why do spies need to learn how to shout and run in small circles?" Metoo inquired.

"I don't know," Dorothy answered. "Maybe it's secret."

"Oh, that makes sense," the young Stryx acknowledged. "All of the biologicals on the stations have secrets, except for the humans, and that's only because you aren't very good at keeping them."

"Am too!" Dorothy rebutted her friend, then immediately turned and fled through the camouflaged opening in the scrap heap and down the welded tunnel.

Metoo floated right behind her, but he couldn't pass in the narrow space without risking giving her a fright, and the regulation ten-second statute of limitations expired long before he could get in front of her to retort with "Are not!" Jeeves had assured Metoo that most of the conversational rules Dorothy taught the young Stryx were fabrications of her overactive imagination, but it was still fun.

Dring was busy welding when the children emerged from the tunnel, and Dorothy, who had grown up with a father who was always doing ship repairs, immediately looked away.

"Don't look, Metoo," she ordered her friend. "You can hurt your eyes."

"I don't really have eyes," Metoo explained for the twenty-sixth time, though his patience was nowhere near spent. He didn't bother telling Dorothy that it was the twenty-sixth time she had warned him about watching a weld in progress because he knew from experience that she wouldn't believe him. Although the ten-year-old girl was extremely bright and had an excellent memory for subjects that interested her, like alien foods and the outfits worn by the dolls in the Little Apple antique store, she treasured her misconceptions with equal tenacity.

Dring sensed the visitors, but he knew it wasn't anything urgent since Metoo didn't interrupt him. The artist kept his attention on the work and continued welding until he finished the bead. Once it was done, he allowed the electrical arc to die with a final sputter and turned to greet his visitors.

"Dorothy! Metoo! What a pleasant surprise." The chubby dinosaur put the tools aside and waddled forward to meet the youngsters. Dorothy ran towards him and threw herself against his soft belly with a thud.

"Mommy said you have to come for dinner," Dorothy informed him.

"The ambassador said to ask Dring if he would come for dinner," Metoo corrected her.

"I know THAT," Dorothy replied in disgust. "But he's more likely to come if he HAS TO."

"You can't argue with her logic," Dring told the little Stryx. "You can tell your Mommy that I accept her invitation or that I shall come as she has ordered. I leave it up to your good judgment."

"Can we go inside, Uncle Dring?" Dorothy pleaded, hanging on to one of the dinosaur's palms. She carefully avoided the blunt claws, which she worried must hurt him since they were often chipped or broken.

"Of course you may," Dring replied graciously. "Thank you for remembering to ask first."

Dorothy raced to the section of the gravity surfer's transparent hull that served as a door and stepped confidently inside. Dring followed and Metoo floated politely behind. A humanoid girl whom Dorothy had never met before was sitting on the bench by the little pond, and she looked up, startled, as Dorothy approached.

"Who are you?" Dorothy asked without hesitation. "Are you Dring's daughter? Do you want to come to dinner?"

"She can't understand you," Dring called from a dozen steps away. "She's a Gem refugee and she doesn't have an implant."

Dorothy carefully studied the unexpected competition for Dring's attention. The girl looked strangely familiar but somehow unfinished to the ambassador's daughter, who was proud of her ability to recognize as many species as her mother.

As Dring approached, Metoo floated out from behind him, and the Gem girl jumped up as if she was about to flee.

"It's just Metoo," Dorothy said, forgetting that the other girl couldn't understand her.

"We don't trust the Stryx," the Gem said shakily. "Please, Dring, make him leave."

"Metoo, could you wait outside?" Dring requested. The Stryx obediently turned and slipped back out of the gravity surfer. "I assure you, young Gem, that the Stryx are entirely harmless, but as you can see, we respect your concerns."

"Why should she understand you and not me?" Dorothy demanded.

"I'm speaking Gem and your new translation implant is giving you the English, just like when she speaks. But you don't speak Gem, so I would have to translate for you."

Dorothy frowned and shook her head in irritation. "Like the translation boxes we used on Kasil?" she asked. Imagining Dring filling the role of that clunky technology made her giggle.

"I would be honored," Dring offered. "I'd feel better if young Gem here could find a friend. It's very rare for clones to leave their crèche worlds before they reach adulthood. She visits me sometimes when the Free Gem are at work."

"What's your name?" Dorothy asked, and then listened critically as Dring repeated the question for her.

"Gem," the girl replied.

"That's not a name," Dorothy scolded her. "I mean like, Sue, Betsy, Matilda, Sarah or Gwendolyn. You know, a REAL name."

Dring repeated Dorothy's words, and the Gem girl looked at him in puzzlement, as if she doubted the accuracy of the translation.

"I could give you my number," the Gem offered. "It's thirty-eight billion, six…"

Dorothy cut the young clone off mid-digit. "If you don't have a real name, we'll have to give you one," she insisted. "Are there any names you like?"

This question brought an even more bewildered look. Finally she answered, "My sisters don't use names. We just know each other."

"Then I'm going to call you Mist," Dorothy declared after a second's hesitation. "It's short for mystery, because your name is a mystery."

"Mist," the girl repeated after Dring translated. "I like it. What's your name?"

"Dorothy," Kelly's daughter replied, and in imitation of her mother's diplomatic introductions, stepped forward to shake the other girl's hand. After a moment, the clone extended her own hand, which Dorothy pumped enthusiastically, putting her free hand over the top like a real politician. Both girls smiled.

"Do you want to play with me and Metoo?" Dorothy asked, now that the formalities were out of the way. Dring took a minor liberty with the translation for the sake of clarity, substituting "my little Stryx friend" for "Metoo."

Mist immediately looked uncomfortable again, but rather than rejecting the proposal out of hand, she asked, "Are you sure he's not working with the bad Gem?"

"Metoo doesn't work for anybody. He's just a kid, like us," Dorothy replied. She either forgot or selectively ignored the fact that her young friend had served two years as the High Priest of Kasil to help save the Kasilian race from extinction.

"I promise that Metoo will be a good friend," Dring added after translating. "I doubt he has ever even met one of your sisters from the Empire. And he can tell you what Dorothy is saying if I'm not there."

"I guess," Mist decided after weighing the options. "But we have to keep it a secret so I don't get into trouble."

"Ooh, I'm very good at keeping secrets," Dorothy said, seizing the other girl's hand again. "Besides, you can tell everybody that Metoo is playing with me and that you're ignoring him."

This formulation put Mist's worries to rest, and the two girls went out to find the little robot, who appeared to be studying Dring's sculptures with great interest. The shape-shifting artist followed behind, and after seeing the Gem accept Metoo's hesitant greeting without getting upset, Dring returned to work, leaving the children to their own devices.

"I like Dring's statues," Mist informed her two new friends. "I asked him to make one of me and he said he would."

"Oh!" Dorothy exclaimed, suddenly jealous. "I never thought of that. I'll do that too." Suddenly, she became shy and asked, "Are you really a clone?"

"Of course," Mist replied after listening to Metoo's translation. "We're all clones, that's where new people come from. Are you sure you're not a clone?"

"I don't think so," Dorothy answered cautiously, floored by the question. "I don't have any sisters. I know that when my baby brother was born, he came out of Mommy's stomach."

"Your mother ate your baby brother?" Mist asked in horror after Metoo finished translating.

"No!" Dorothy protested. "The stork put him in there. It's complicated, though. We can't understand until we're older."

"That's alright," Mist said. "Lots of things are complicated. Sometimes, I think the adults don't really know the answers so they just say that."

"That's what I think," Dorothy agreed excitedly. "Do they do the same thing to you, Metoo?"

Metoo successfully negotiated the tricky task of translating Dorothy's words and posing a question to himself simultaneously.

"No, the grown-up Stryx always explain everything to me in detail," he confessed. "But sometimes I don't really understand it all even if the math works out. Especially the multiverse stuff."

The two girls nodded in sympathy as Dring's welding arced and spat in the background.

"Let's go see what they're doing outside," Dorothy suggested. This time, Metoo led the way through the scrapmound tunnel with the two girls in noisy pursuit.

The recruits in the designated training camp area were now paired off by twos, sitting cross-legged on blankets with a little mound of trade goods in front of each person. Lynx stalked up and down the rows of blankets shouting advice and encouragement.

"Come on, hold that tea kettle like you never want to part with it. You look like you're dying for a chance to give it away. That's right, even a box full of shredded paper has value if you run into somebody with a hamster. What? No, I don't know if the aliens have hamsters, it's just an example. Hi, Dorothy. Metoo. Who's your new friend?"

"This is Mist," Dorothy replied confidently. "Mist, this is Aunty Lynx." Metoo hung close to the Gem's side and translated in an undertone.

"Hello, Mist," Lynx greeted the girl. "Do you want to play being a trader?"

"Yes, please," Mist answered.

Lynx shook out a new blanket for the girls and motioned them to sit. Then she quickly surveyed the group of agent trainees who were trying to learn enough about trading for a cover story, and singled out the man with the largest pile of goods.

"Bart, you've done this before," she addressed him.

"Three years on the fringe," Bart acknowledged.

"Alright, I'm giving you a handicap," Lynx declared, sweeping most of the goods from his pile into an empty box. "Carry on."

Dorothy squealed when Lynx emptied the box onto the center of the blanket she shared with Mist. The items were primarily kitchen utensils that she recognized, and in fact, most of them had been borrowed from the McAllister's occasional-use drawer.

"Just divide these up evenly between the two of you," Lynx said. Then she added, "Metoo. Make sure Dorothy doesn't cheat. I'll be back in a bit to help you get started."

Dorothy immediately took command, doing a one-for-me, one-for-you division, under the watchful 'not exactly' eyes of Metoo.

"What are all these humans doing?" Mist asked.

"They're training to be spies," Dorothy replied immediately.

Rather than translating, Metoo said to Dorothy, "But it's supposed to be secret."

"You're right!" the ambassador's daughter declared, her eyes going wide at her blunder. "Make her promise to keep it secret first."

Mist readily agreed to keep the secret, after which Metoo translated Dorothy's original answer. The Gem girl didn't seem the least bit surprised.

"All Gem are spies," Mist commented. "We don't need any special training. In the crèche, one in every ten sisters is a Big Sister, and she reports everything you do wrong to the teacher. I had a doll once that I hand-stitched clothes for, but Big Sister told the teacher, and the teacher said that the clothes weren't Gem and burned them."

"Did you cry?" Dorothy asked.

"Yes," Mist replied. "Then Big Sister told the teacher that I cried, and the teacher said that wasn't Gem and she beat me."

"That's terrible," Metoo said of his own accord. "Nobody gets beaten in Stryx school."

"Yes, you should join us Monday," Dorothy said enthusiastically.

"I don't have any money," Mist confessed. "Maybe Dring will give me some. He's very nice."

"You don't need any money," Dorothy explained. "You just have to do some barter work for the Stryx in return."

"What work do you do?" Mist asked curiously.

"My job is to play with Metoo," Dorothy reported proudly. "It's a lot of work, though, because he never forgets anything, so I have to make up new rules all of the time. Maybe you can be my helper."

"Are you girls ready to barter?" Lynx asked, having completed another critical round of the blankets.

"Yes, Aunty Lynx," Dorothy responded. "Who goes first?"

"Why don't you?" Lynx replied. "Ask your friend for something from her pile."

"Can I have your nutcracker?" Dorothy asked, pointing to the elaborate device. As soon as Metoo translated, the Gem girl handed it over.

"No," Lynx interrupted the transaction, handing the nutcracker back. "Mist, the point of bartering is to get something in return. In a good barter deal, each of you gets something that's more valuable to you than the item you're giving away. That way, you're both happy. Have you ever shopped in a market?"

"Only on Union Station," the girl replied, after Metoo completed translating the instructions. "We don't have markets back home. Everything comes from the Gem warehouse, and everybody is supposed to get the same things."

"Do they?" Dorothy asked.

"In crèche, the Big Sisters get more, and they also take things from their little sisters not to tell on us," Mist replied matter-of-factly. "I didn't have anything left to give my Big Sister, and I knew she was going to report me to the teacher for talking to the janitor, so I stowed away on an inspection ship and ended up here."

"You should tell the Stryx on them!" Dorothy cried, then decided to do it herself. "Metoo. Tell the other Stryx to make the Big Sisters stop being mean!"

"I'm sorry, Dorothy," Metoo replied. "I already did tell them, but the Gem Empire is an independent civilization and the older Stryx won't interfere with their internal affairs."

"The Stryx can't solve all of the problems of the galaxy," Lynx told Dorothy. "But you can help your friend right now by teaching her to barter."

"I'm still going to tell Mommy," Dorothy muttered darkly.

"What would you like from Dorothy's pile in return for your nutcracker," Lynx asked Mist, to advance the negotiations. The young Gem leaned forward to study the items on offer, obviously puzzled by their function.

"Can I have the chocolate divider?" she asked shyly, pointing at the hardboiled-egg slicer.

"It's really a chocolate divider?" Dorothy asked in surprise. "Mommy tried using it on hardboiled eggs one time, but the slices broke or stuck together. She said something about it not working right."

"It's for chocolate eggs," Mist told her. "We use it to share them because chocolate is so precious. I always get the end cuts because I'm little."

"I don't know," Dorothy responded, thinking hard. "A chocolate slicer should be worth more than a nutcracker, don't you agree?"

Lynx smiled and moved on to help some of the less promising trainees. Metoo had a fun time translating Dorothy and Mist's increasingly complicated swap scenarios, including deals that featured objects not present on the blanket which he suspected both girls were simply making up. In the end, Dorothy received a nutcracker, a glass orange-juicer and a peppermill, in exchange for the egg slicer and a cheese grater, which Mist intended to use to shred chocolate over everything.

Seven

In accordance with the ambassador's request, Kelly arrived at the Drazen embassy's meeting room ten minutes before the scheduled multi-species consultation was scheduled to begin. It was the third meeting of an informal group of ambassadors who had been gathering to discuss the rapidly developing situation with the Gem refugees on the station and elsewhere. Despite their differences, the stable species of the galaxy had long since learned how to temporarily put aside their every-day rivalries when something that threatened their bottom line appeared on the horizon.

"Did you already sell the human block for the election?" Bork asked after a quick greeting. "I didn't see it listed on the tote board."

"What are you talking about?"

"For the Carnival election," Bork replied. "I'm sure you know that station residents can vote for as many candidates as they choose, and it's traditional for ambassadors to trade or sell the votes from their species. I assume that you aren't interested in winning yourself since you skipped all of the pre-Carnival meetings."

"I was busy with the baby," Kelly excused herself, having found that most of the station species would accept the duties of motherhood as an excuse for anything, since they didn't want to risk giving cultural offence. "Humans don't sell votes so I couldn't deliver them if I wanted to. And what's this tote board you're talking about?"

"The off-world betting parlor near the conference center is the traditional clearing house for votes, since they have all of the secure hardware and register capacity in place. Are you sure you can't deliver the human vote? The Drazen embassy uses the money we get selling votes to fund a Carnival picnic."

"I'm not comfortable with the whole vote-selling concept," Kelly confessed. "It's a crime back on Earth, you know."

"Interesting," Bork mused. "My impression from the Grenouthian documentary on human democracy was that elections were once a major part of the economy on Earth. I'm not sure I've ever heard of a species that made vote-selling illegal, though the opposite is somewhat common."

"The opposite?" Kelly repeated. "You mean there are species who require that votes be bought and sold?"

"It's a form of social insurance," Bork explained. "The poor can't realistically hope to get elected to anything, so at least they can get some benefit out of the process. I seem to remember that the Frunge used to hold elections every ten days or so, just their method of spreading the wealth."

"Why did you ask about the human vote, Bork?" Kelly inquired. "Are you actually trying to get elected Carnival King?"

"Of course," Bork replied. "There hasn't been a Drazen elected in many generations, and our residents would appreciate a cycle of free rent, not to mention bragging rights. But the Verlocks and the Vergallians are much better at managing the vote-buying market than we are, especially the countdown deals when the prices go crazy."

"Do I want to ask?" Kelly said with a grimace.

"There's a party at the off-world betting parlor on Election Day, and everybody counts down the last ten update cycles," Bork explained enthusiastically. "I wasn't an ambassador at the previous election, but I was on the station and snuck into the hall. Some species wait until the last possible moment to release their vote tallies, and they can change the outcome of a close election. Of course, if it's a landslide because somebody, uh, bypasses the technology, those votes go unsold. So it's always a gamble."

"Making the election an even better fit for the betting parlor," Kelly commented dryly, but Bork twisted his thumb and sixth finger in front of his lips, the Drazen version of "Shhh!"

"I hope I'm not interrupting anything," ambassador Czeros said, settling onto his root-like feet after tiptoeing into the room. "I'm sure the two of you wouldn't leave your old Frunge friend out of the discussion if you were swapping votes."

"The humans don't trade or sell votes," Bork informed Czeros, spreading his hands in the equivalent of a human shrug.

"Maybe you didn't offer enough," Czeros suggested. "Not selling excess votes is like throwing away a half-full bottle of wine. What if I guaranteed a full swap? A vote for me is a vote for you, and I'll pledge my double vote for human competitors in three Carnival contests of your choice if I become King."

"That's a very generous offer, Czeros, but I can't tell the humans to vote for somebody," Kelly explained.

"Don't they want you to win?" Czeros asked in shock.

"Yes, I'm sure they do," Kelly replied. "They even have a committee to get me elected, but we don't believe in buying votes."

"Then how did you settle elections back on your Earth?" Czeros asked curiously.

"Advertising," Kelly replied. The two alien ambassadors favored her with reproachful looks. "It's not the same thing as buying votes outright," she protested. The truth was that Kelly had left Earth at twenty and she had never voted in an election, so she wasn't really sure if they even held them anymore. She'd have to remember to ask her mother.

"Hello, Crute," Bork greeted the Dollnick ambassador as the towering alien ducked through the doorway. "I was just looking over the ballot for the five elective Carnival events, and I see that you're pushing paddle-cup-mitt-ball."

"Can I count on the Drazen vote?" Crute asked.

"The thing is, Crute, it seems that it's impossible to play the game unless you have four hands," Bork replied apologetically. "But I hope you will support the Drazen proposal to add Treyball."

"Isn't that the game with the net that requires each player to use two racquets while holding a basket above the head?" the Frunge ambassador asked acidly. "Those of us without a tentacle may find it difficult to compete."

"But our friends the Dollnicks can play and still have a free hand to use as a spare," Bork pointed out. "Besides, how many of the station species can compete at micro-fracture rock climbing? Not all of us have a network of roots for feet and climbing vines for hair."

"Why do I get the impression that all of the elective events being proposed favor species with certain anatomical advantages?" Kelly asked diplomatically. "Wouldn't it be more fun if you recommended events in which everybody could compete?"

"You sound like your assistant today, the one who would probably be happier teaching children," Bork replied. "And what was that event that humans are proposing?"

"Caber toss," Kelly replied readily. "I never heard of it before myself, but my husband says that anybody with the strength and a good sense of balance can compete."

"The Frunge are voting for it," Czeros informed her. "Keep micro-fracture rock climbing in mind. I recall seeing a documentary that showed how humans would quickly climb anything to get away from predators not too long ago. There's no better preparation in life than latent ability."

"It's a shame you all lack latent ability in the looks department," proclaimed Ambassador Apria as she strode into the room. A typical flawless beauty of the Vergallian upper class, she was the latest to take a turn as the top diplomat for her people on Union Station. Ambassadors from the Hundred Worlds only served a short rotation, approximately two human years.

"And you, Apria, look lovely today," Bork replied amiably. "I believe if you competed in Treyball, the other contestants would be so blinded by your beauty that you'd win without breaking a sweat."

"Try that line on the human," Apria retorted. "Though since you've brought up the subject of the elective events, I'd like to point out that anybody with a sense of rhythm and a love of music can compete in the ballroom dancing we've proposed."

"And how many hours a day does the typical Vergallian youth spend practicing?" Crute asked sweetly.

"Sentients, sentients," boomed the Verlock ambassador as he shuffled slowly into the room. "The elective events won't be chosen today. I am here to discuss Gem."

As soon as the Verlock was through the doorway, the Grenouthian and Horten ambassadors who had been stuck behind him in the corridor entered.

"Looks like everybody is here except for the Chert," Kelly commented. The empty seat at the end of the table suddenly filled itself with a Chert, an invisibility projector on his shoulder.

"Sorry. Old habits die hard," the Chert ambassador explained. "Speaking of which, I hope you'll all consider voting for our hide-and-seek as an elective event. The children love it."

"Please, everybody be seated," Bork announced. "It looks like we'll be starting on time today, of all the things."

"Are there no refreshments?" Czeros asked, drawing a wave of muttered support from the other ambassadors.

"We sent out for wine and fruit salad from a human shop in the Little Apple, since that seems to agree with everybody," Bork replied. "Now, can we begin?"

"Has Ambassador McAllister met with the Free Gem?" Ambassador Ortha inquired. The Horten was much better at controlling his skin color than most of his compatriots, but at the moment, he was showing white patches of curiosity.

"I did meet with their representatives on the station, and I have a follow-up meeting scheduled," Kelly answered for herself. "Unfortunately, the Free Gem have all had their implants removed as a security precaution and they wouldn't allow Stryx translation, so my side of the conversation was somewhat limited."

"They don't trust the Stryx and can't understand humans," Apria commented. "Maybe the clones aren't such a nasty lot after all."

"Did you get any information about their support in the Gem Empire?" asked the Grenouthian ambassador, whose name Kelly had never learned.

"No. I didn't want to seem pushy, and I'm not sure the one who spoke a little English would have understood me if I had asked," Kelly replied. She tried to remember what had been discussed. "They all liked my baby."

"We have some visibility into the Gem Empire," the Verlock ambassador droned slowly, patting the table like a drum head in an attempt to speed himself up. "The Gem colony worlds and outposts are complaining of shortages. We speculate their supply system is compromised, but we don't know if this is due to the defections, or contributing to them."

"Very interesting, Ambassador," Bork said respectfully. "Does anybody else have information to share?"

"You all know that a segment of our population broke away a long time ago to become, well, freebooters outside of Stryx space," Ortha said. The tunnel network Hortens were notoriously sensitive about the fact that their estranged cousins were overrepresented in the piracy demographic, but of course, they were notoriously sensitive about everything. "It seems that Gem outposts and mining colonies are increasingly left unprotected, and surprisingly, some of the Gem whose facilities get raided are begging to join with their attackers."

"When the fabric of a centralized society begins to weaken, it frays first around the edges," Czeros commented. "We have no particular insight into the Gem Empire as the very concept of cloning is abhorrent to us, but just before this meeting, I heard report of a Gem military vessel trying to surrender itself to one of our frigates out there, somewhere," he concluded with a vague gesture at the ceiling.

"Was their surrender accepted?" Kelly asked urgently, suddenly fearing the worst.

"We are not at war," Czeros answered. "I'm told that our captain, against the wishes of his crew I may add, transferred emergency supplies to the Gem vessel. But he wisely avoided committing the Frunge to a course of action by doing anything official."

"So we can agree that their empire is under some stress," Bork said. "Our own intelligence has detected an uptick in official Gem selling activity in various markets. Unfortunately for the Gem, they have little that anybody wants. A culture dedicated to the cloning and support of a single individual tends to lose touch with the galactic trends."

The door to the conference room slid open, and the ambassadors were startled to see two Gem in uniforms.

"Please remain in your seats," the older Gem said as she entered the room. For a moment, Kelly wondered if they were being taken hostage by some splinter group. Then the woman placed a napkin in front of the Grenouthian ambassador, and they all realized that the Gem were working for a human caterer.

"Serendipitous," Bork muttered to Kelly. "Do you think we should take advantage and ask a few questions?"

"Don't forget the language barrier," Kelly whispered back. "Their employer must use a translation box, unless these two have been working long enough to learn some English."

"Try saying something to them," Bork suggested.

Kelly hesitated, then addressed the clone who was placing a large oval tray of citrus fruit on the table. The peeled fruit had all been separated into sections and arranged in flower patterns of pink, orange, yellow and green.

"Excuse me," Kelly said to the woman, who had stepped back from the table to view the results of her work. "Do you speak English?"

The clone cleared her throat and said, "Gratuities accepted."

Bork grumbled and dug in his pocket, extracting a twenty-cred piece which he deposited in the clone's outstretched palm. "I'm the host. That's for everybody."

The Gem didn't understand Drazen, but she smiled and said "Thank you." Twenty creds would buy a lot of chocolate if you got up early enough on delivery day. She and her sister pushed the empty bus floater back into the corridor and headed for their next job.

Kelly didn't want to be the first to ruin the artistic arrangement of citrus wedges, but her fellow ambassadors had no such compunctions. The discussion was put on hold for a moment as they all began to inhale the fruit. The Dollnick was particularly effective, grabbing pieces with all four hands and throwing them towards his mouth in a continual arc. Czeros concentrated on the sole cheese platter.

"These are excellent," Bork informed Kelly. "Best oranges I've ever had."

Kelly tried one of the wedges pointed out by the Drazen ambassador and her face immediately puckered up. "This is a lemon," she sputtered.

"It really is delicious," Apria concurred with the Drazen. "I find it quite droll that when you humans finally produce a really tasty fruit, you can't eat it."

71

"If there are no objections, I will speak while you feed," the Verlock ambassador slowly intoned from the end of the table. He couldn't compete for fruit with the fast-twitch muscles of the grabby diplomats, and didn't care for high water content foods in any case.

"Mmph, please," Bork yielded the floor.

"Gem is both an individual and a species. A centrally planned empire with a rigid system for raising and educating young clones has exacerbated isolation from the larger galactic economy. A combination of vanity and paranoia has led the Gem to believe that their system is superior to all others, that progress is equivalent to treason, and that everyone else stands against them."

"That much is true," Czeros interrupted.

"Verlock analysts are in agreement that the Gem Empire is on a course to self-destruction. But the current wave of defections was not predicted by our modeling of the situation, which included as a fundamental assumption that the Gem are too similarly programmed, through both genetics and upbringing, to revolt against themselves."

"Nature versus nurture," Kelly commented.

"Nature and nurture," Czeros corrected her.

"Clones are hardly natural," Apria interjected.

"The point being, we were wrong," the Verlock continued as if no interruptions had taken place. "It is unclear to us why we were wrong. Gem is neither evolving nor changing through selective breeding. While Gem technology is largely frozen in time at the level of their last civil war, their mastery of the cloning process is undoubtedly sufficient to prevent large-scale replication errors that could explain the statistical anomalies in individual behavior."

72

"Wait a second," Kelly said, holding up her hand to stop the Verlock. "I don't know anything about replication technology, but both my dinner with the Gem ambassador a few years ago and my recent meeting with the Free Gem were enough to convince me that they are individuals, even though they are clones."

"Did that make sense in your native language, or are you interviewing for a job as an oracle?" Apria asked icily. "According to my translation implant, you just said that the clones are clones even though they are clones."

"What's the word for 'clone' in your native language?" Kelly asked.

"Gem," the Vergallian ambassador replied. Most of the diplomats around the table shook their heads in agreement.

"But our Verlock colleague and myself are differentiating between Gem as a species and cloning as a replication process," Kelly pointed out.

"With all due respect to our esteemed Verlock friend, he speaks so slowly that by the time he finishes a sentence, I forget how it started," Crute replied. "Besides, what difference does it make? We're all agreed that cloning is a nasty business, though I have to admit, they make a fantastic fruit platter."

"My point is that most of you have a preconceived notion that the forty billion or so Gem are indivisible as one, while I've come to see them as a dysfunctional family."

"The human ambassador is correct," Apria said, beaming a smile that made Kelly feel a chill down to her toes. "Due to her unique understanding of the Gem situation, I move that we appoint Mrs. McAllister the permanent chair of this committee rather than rotating duties. She can handle any necessary communications between the Gem, Free Gem, Stryx and whatnot. I know that my own time would be better spent preparing an acceptance speech for my inevitable election as Carnival Queen."

"Agreed," chorused several of the other ambassadors, hastily rising from their seats.

Kelly glared at Czeros, who was trying to slip out unnoticed behind the large Dollnick ambassador.

"I have a, uh, thing, with, uh, you know," he apologized, then turned and fled.

"What did I do wrong, Bork?" Kelly complained. "One minute, the ambassadors were sharing intelligence information, the next minute, they dumped the whole thing on me and ran for the door."

"Slide me the cracker platter," Bork replied sadly, pointing at the former cheese platter that had been denuded of cheese. "If I had ordered more food they would still be here."

"So now I'm supposed to make all of the decisions on my own responsibility, without the support of the other species?"

"They were just getting even with you for suggesting that they didn't understand the Gem, a race we've all been in contact with for longer than humans have practiced agriculture," Bork explained. "As chairman, or chairwoman, you can still call a meeting at any time."

"It's getting to the point that I'm afraid to open my mouth in meetings," Kelly grumbled. "You know, our EarthCent committee made me Minister of Intelligence just for being at the wrong place at the wrong time."

Eight

"So you're all sneaking off together for some kind of male bonding trip?" Blythe asked skeptically.

"There are only two human colony worlds outside the tunnel network and both of them are completely independent of Earth," Clive explained. "We don't know anything about their defensive readiness, and if the Gem situation worsens and the clone military goes berserk, those colonies could be attractive targets."

"Kibbutz and Bits," Blythe continued dismissively. "Together they sound like one of those weird product names that marketers used to come up with back on Earth."

"We assume that Kibbutz is a collective world established along socialist guidelines that prohibit personal property," Clive said. "Bits is a planet of technology geeks, a place where people plug in, turn on and tune in to virtual reality. Neither world has an EarthCent presence and we really don't know much about them. Just another area where our intelligence is falling short."

"Bits produces a lot of interactive games and they're one of the big brand names," Paul chimed in. "I've also heard they do contract programming for mechanicals and other dumb devices."

"I understand why Clive has to go, he's the head of EarthCent Intelligence and the captain of the Effterii,"

Aisha interrupted. "And Woojin is your new defense expert, I get that. But why do you have to go?" she demanded of her husband.

"I'm sort of the envoy to the geeks," he replied self-consciously. "And the ambassador wanted me to go for some reason." Wrapping himself in the non-existent EarthCent flag usually worked with Aisha.

"His mother wanted him to go so that Jeeves would go too," Blythe interpreted for Aisha. "I'll bet she's afraid that Jeeves will ignore the older Stryx and fix the election in her favor if he's here on the station. He'd probably do it at the last minute, just for a joke."

"And why is Thomas going?" Aisha asked.

"We've got two ex-mercenaries, a former Nova champion and an unstable Stryx, off on a jaunt across the galaxy in a sentient alien spaceship," Blythe explained. "I thought it would be a good idea for Thomas to go along to supervise. He was our best babysitter before he caught the secret agent bug."

"Well, that's all settled then," Clive declared, putting an arm around Blythe's shoulders. The two couples were meeting for lunch at the latest ice cream parlor to open in the Little Apple, a retro restaurant that featured high-backed booths that were ideal for snuggling. How they earned enough selling ice cream to pay for the inefficient use of floor space was anybody's guess.

"I still think you're trying to sneak off to get out of having to judge any more contestants," Aisha accused her husband.

"That's not true!" Paul protested energetically. "I enjoyed meeting all of those artists, and they did some really interesting work."

"But you were supposed to at least narrow down the list of candidates. The rest of us took a lot of criticism for making some hard choices when we started picking finalists from our groups. You just kicked the can down the road for another week, and now you aren't going to be here to pick it up!"

"That's another reason for me to go," Paul pointed out. "I'm not any good at judging that subjective stuff. If it was just a question of picking which painting was the reddest, which drawing looked like a real bowl of fruit, which sculpture would be worth the most as scrap metal, I'm your man. But everybody expected me to see things that just weren't there, and when I didn't, they tried to talk me into it. You can't explain art, at least not to me. And if the work can't speak for itself, what's the point?"

"You're just lucky that Shaina and Brinda agreed to help out," Aisha told him. In addition to leaving Jeeves at loose ends, the end of the auction season meant that Peter Hadad's workaholic daughters were back on the station, and they had happily stepped into the role of special troubleshooters for the human Carnival committee. Since Aisha and the three remaining committee members all had full-time jobs, they had willingly handed over the organizational work, though they were still stuck judging the weekend trials.

"So where is the rest of your merry band?" Blythe asked her husband. The men were leaving the station after lunch, and she wasn't in any hurry to see her husband off, so she was nursing her coffee milkshake. Her initial impulse had been to invite herself along on the improvised mission, but Lynx was now filling in as Union Station's cultural attaché in addition to her recruit-training duties. It wouldn't have been fair to run off with Clive and Thomas, who were numbers one and four in the organization, leaving Lynx as the only senior member of EarthCent Intelligence in charge during what could easily turn into their first crisis.

"Woojin is helping Joe get the Nova ready for our trip," Paul explained. "The tug will fit in the Effterii's hold, and we can use it as a shuttle to get down to the colony worlds. Jeeves said something about visiting the Stryx storerooms, and Thomas asked me to ping him ten minutes before we leave, just in case he loses track of time."

"Did you get all of that, Aisha?" Blythe asked.

"I think so," the young diplomat replied cautiously. "Woojin and Joe are doing maintenance, Jeeves is getting supplies, and Thomas is meditating or something."

"Woojin and Joe are loading the Nova with beer, Jeeves is loading himself with weapons, and Thomas is in a club on some deck where the species call it night, dancing with Chance," Blythe corrected her. "Am I right, Paul?"

"You make it sound like we're all trying to get away with something," he mumbled.

Two hours later, as the main bay doors of the Effterii slid shut behind the Nova and the two pilots unstrapped their safety harnesses, Paul turned to Clive and exclaimed, "I can't believe we got away with it. I thought I was going to be stuck another weekend trying to referee a bunch of crazy artists."

"Try auctioning the stuff off sometime," Jeeves commented. "The bidders don't even look at the works, they're just buying the name. You could pick a used napkin out of the trash, sign it 'Jonathan Posturnack,' put it in a frame, and I'll auction it off for a million creds."

"Posturnack," Woojin said, joining in from one of the two fold-out jump seats behind the command chairs. "I think I recognize that name. Is he the one who rounded up a bunch of starving feral cats in Paris, poured different colors of paint on them, and used hidden cameras to shoot an immersive when he released them in a fancy restaurant?"

"Yes, the height of human artistic endeavor," Jeeves remarked.

"Oh, I saw that too," Paul said. "It was kind of funny."

"It sounds like the kind of activity I was always instructed not to let the children engage in when I was babysitting for humans," Thomas commented, freeing himself from the safety harness on the other jump seat. "No playing with food or paint was at the very top of the list."

"Did we just jump?" Woojin suddenly asked in surprise.

"Yup, we're approaching Kibbutz orbit now, stealth mode," Clive replied with a grin. "I've been practicing with the Key, and the Effterii is pretty tuned in to my thought patterns now. I can transmit simple instructions without even moving my lips."

"When you said the Effterii jumps were practically instantaneous, I was thinking along the lines of minutes or hours instead of days or weeks." Woojin said. "That felt different, like something between a jump and a tunnel transit. I've been through hundreds of both, and that was more muted than a jump, but with more wrongness than a tunnel."

"Wrongness?" Thomas inquired. "I don't believe I've ever heard tunnel transits described that way."

"I know exactly what he means," Paul said. "A minute ago, I could have pointed you in the direction of Union Station, even though we're inside the Nova in Zero-G in the hold of the Effterii. I might have pointed the wrong way, but I would have felt like I knew where it was. Now I feel like I'd have to look down just to see where my feet are."

"You know why we stretch out tunnel transits for biologicals," Jeeves reminded his friend. "Your brains don't adapt well to traveling light years in an instant. The Effterii method is closer to Stryx tunnel technology than to the crude jump tricks employed by biologicals. This ship moves around the galaxy by hopping through the multiverse, rather than punching holes."

"This'll teach me to go on a trip without asking about the engines," Woojin remarked ruefully. "Are you saying that rather than going from point A to point B using a bunch of math I don't understand, this ship has gone from point A in one universe to point B in another universe using a bunch of math I don't understand?"

"That's one interpretation," Jeeves replied cheerfully. "The equations allow for an infinite number of universes branching from every new event, but even if we've swapped universes rather than returning to our own, I don't see the problem if we can't tell the difference."

"That's because you're not married," Paul groaned. "Please, whether this is our own universe or not, when we get back to Union Station, nobody mention the part about how we may not be us to Aisha."

"Don't forget that the sudden change is likely interfering with your mental processes and leading you to think morbid thoughts," Jeeves added helpfully. "Now, do you want me to initiate contact with the humans on the surface, or shall we wait until the Nova exits the hold and becomes visible to their planetary defense systems?"

"We may as well keep the Effterii as our ace in the hole," Clive replied thoughtfully. "If they're suspicious about a tug without a jump drive appearing out of no-where, we can always blame it on you, Jeeves."

"Will you be able to communicate with the Effterii from the surface of the planet?" Thomas asked.

"I think so," Clive replied. "As long as I've got the Key, it doesn't seem to matter how far away I am. The way the ship explained it, the Key is a sort of a sympathetic crystal and its mate is built into the Effterii's brain. Maybe it uses quantum coupling like the Stryx controllers, I didn't really understand."

None of the travelers could actually have explained why they were floating about the crowded bridge rather than remaining strapped into their seats. It was just something you did after a jump. Of the five, Thomas had the least practice moving about in Zero-G, but unlike the humans, he had bought an upgrade for his feet, so he didn't need magnetic cleats to walk on the deck, or any other surface for that matter.

"We're going to look like a bunch of nut jobs on the comm screen," Clive commented, observing his team. "Everybody holding onto something? Paul, can you ease us out?"

"Just takes a nudge from the nav jets," Paul reported. But he buckled himself back into the pilot's chair to be safe, and then took them out of the Effterii's hold with a series of small bumps.

"Hmm," Jeeves mused. "I'd think we must have appeared on their radar as soon as we cleared the hold, but I'm not picking up any signals activity on the surface."

"Maybe nobody's watching the store," Woojin suggested. "Best detection technology in the galaxy isn't worth much if you turn off the alarms and go to a party."

"I'm going to try waking them up," Clive said. "How do I open a general broadcast channel on this thing, Paul?"

"Here, I'll do it," Paul said, tapping the command pad on the central console. "We're knocking, let's see if anybody answers the door."

A minute went by. Then two minutes, then five.

"Any signs of trouble down there, Jeeves?"

"Nothing obvious," the Stryx replied. "Place is crawling with biologicals, if you'll pardon the expression, though they seem to be spread pretty thin, no major concentrations."

"Should we just land?" Paul asked Clive, who was officially in command of the mission.

"Why don't we do a couple of low orbits first, to learn what we can from space. I'm tempted to call the Effterii down closer to scan for defensive systems, which will give us a head-start when we talk to their people."

"I can do that for you," Jeeves offered matter-of-factly. "There's the typical radar net that should have triggered a response by now since it's bouncing off us even as I speak. Let's see, some automated anti-asteroid emplacements on satellites, standard stuff that probably came with the contract for the planet. Nope, that's it for this hemisphere anyway. Maybe there's something around the other side."

Thirty minutes later, it was apparent that Kibbutz didn't have anything on the surface that could stop an aggressive raid, much less a Gem military vessel. Just when Clive was about to give up on raising a response from the inhabitants, the main viewer came on. A young boy wearing a crudely woven straw hat and homespun clothing that was colored with a pale blue dye squinted at them critically.

"Who are you?" he asked in English.

"We're from EarthCent," Clive replied. "We're here to talk to your government."

"Don't got one," the boy replied. "My Pa is milking now, but I can get him for you after if you want."

Clive looked at Paul and made a subtle cut-throat gesture up around his chest.

"Volume off," Paul said. "I don't think the kid is joking."

"I know it's supposed to be an agrarian paradise, but does it make sense that they'd turn their spaceport into a farm?" Woojin asked.

"I'm good with children," Thomas said. "Let me try."

Clive shrugged and Paul tapped the pad on the console.

"What's your name?" Thomas asked the boy.

"Brian," he replied sulkily. He had seen their lips moving and knew they had been talking behind his back without even getting him to turn around first.

"How old are you, Brian?" Thomas followed up.

"I'm nine," the boy replied, becoming interested in the conversation. "And my birthday is next week!"

"Maybe we can bring you a birthday present," Thomas continued. "Is there something special you want?"

The boy thought for a moment, and then he asked, "Space stuff?"

"Sure, if your parents allow it," the artificial person replied.

"Never mind," the boy said sourly. "So, are you coming to visit, or are you just going to sit up there in orbit and make fun of us, like most of the other ships that stop by?"

"We'd like to come visit," Thomas answered, with a glance at Clive. "Do you know where we can land?"

"Right here is the only place with ramps and stuff, though I guess you can land anywhere if you got your own," the boy responded. "Pa charges fifty creds a day to use the old spaceport. Don't scorch any of the fields on the edges or he'll be mad."

"I think we can manage that," Paul cut in on the conversation. "How close to the landing field are you?"

"I'm right in front of it, in the tower," Brian replied. "Can't you see it out the windows behind me?"

The humans all stared, and sure enough, now that the boy mentioned it, they could see that the view through the dirty windows behind him was of a large expanse of broken concrete. The faint sound of clanging came over the comm and the boy jumped out of his seat.

"I gotta go," he said hastily. "See you later, maybe."

As Brian moved out of the picture, Jeeves said, "Allow me." The image changed suddenly, replaced by a bird's eye view of the old spaceport, centered on a tilting control tower that looked like it was built on shock absorbers. A small boy ran out the bottom and sprinted between the arrays of randomly pointed solar panels in the direction of a human figure, which was carrying something in its hand. The image zoomed in further and they saw it was a girl with a large hand-bell.

"Breakfast time, I reckon," Woojin declared with a grin, showing off his mastery of the old English vernacular. "Maybe my years of watching those Western movies is finally going to pay off."

"I don't remember cowboys being socialists," Paul objected.

"I've read some of that history," Clive ventured, not mentioning that he had read it recently while trying to catch up with the childhood education he had missed. "Some of the native tribes were pretty communal."

84

"Ahem," Jeeves said, zooming the image back out. Most of the disused spaceport was surrounded by scrub, but the end near the abandoned control tower showed a patchwork of pasture, along with some smaller fields that featured rows of plantings. A long, low, cow shed entered the picture not far from the house, but as Jeeves continued zooming out, nothing of interest came into view until the house and shed looked like game pieces. At that point, another homestead appeared, but it must have been a brisk hour's walk from the first.

"Can there be such a thing as antisocial socialists?" Thomas asked.

"Probably," Clive replied, "I doubt that's the case here, though. Let's take a couple more spins around the planet before landing, Paul. Maybe there's a bigger concentration of people somewhere, even if it's just a village."

Nine

Kelly left Samuel at home for her second face-to-face with the clones. The meeting took place at the end of the workday on the former Gem ag deck undergoing conversion to a parkland, and when she stepped out of the lift tube, the ambassador was momentarily taken aback by the thousands of clones tramping in her direction out of the gently curving fields.

"Over here," called the green-haired Gem leader, who had obviously been waiting for her. Kelly gladly moved away from the lift tubes, and after a brief greeting, the clone led her off on a trodden dirt path. "We prepared a place in the fields so nobody can come upon us by surprise," the woman said.

Kelly keyed on the external voice box she'd borrowed from EarthCent's first-contact supplies and subvoced, "I have brought our translation device so we can speak freely today."

"It isn't a Stryx?" the Gem asked suspiciously.

"No, it's just a machine," Kelly reassured her. "But that is one of the things I wanted to talk to you about, and maybe it's best we get it out of the way before we reach your sisters. You've explained to me that you've been lied to all your lives and don't know who to trust, but I want to assure you that the Stryx are not allies of the Gem Empire."

"The Empire has used the tunnel network since the be-ginning," the Gem replied angrily.

"The Stryx allow everybody who plays by their rules access to the tunnels," Kelly replied. "They don't want to tell biologicals how to run their worlds, and even on the stations, they try not to interfere with our internal affairs. But I know for a fact that they've told your sisters in the Empire that the Free Gem on the stations can't be touched."

The Gem didn't reply immediately, but neither did she look convinced, so Kelly tried again.

"The Stryx will only interfere with a species on the tun-nel network if it attempts to enslave or eradicate other civilizations," Kelly explained. "The Gem civil wars and your current Empire are seen as internal Gem affairs, and the Stryx respect that you are mature biologicals capable of making your own decisions. Do you want the Stryx to start picking your leaders for you like they do for—er, do you?"

"Like who?" the green-haired Gem inquired. "Are there species the Stryx treat like children?"

Kelly blushed and mumbled something about her big mouth under her breath. An awkward silence ensued.

"It's complicated," the human ambassador subvoced finally, the external voice box translating her words fluent-ly. "Humans don't really have leaders beyond our home world these days, we're basically guests most places in the galaxy. The Stryx sort of pick the new employees for EarthCent, like I was recruited over twenty years ago, and we aren't really in charge of that much. But everybody goes along with it because we owe the Stryx for gifting us with interstellar space travel before we developed it ourselves. It's similar with the other species the Stryx have fostered."

"But why you and not us?" the Gem insisted.

"Because the Stryx decided we were too stupid to manage things for ourselves," Kelly admitted. "They determined that we were on the verge of a global economic collapse that would have led to such terrible conditions that we would likely have gone extinct. And remember, we weren't on the tunnel network at the time, so it's a different set of rules."

"I understand now," the clone replied. "Some of our political indoctrination referred to humans as Stryx pets, but I assumed it was anti-human propaganda."

"The important thing that I want you to understand is that you can trust the Stryx," Kelly continued, wincing at the characterization of humanity. "They may not help you in your struggle against your sisters, I can't speak for them any more than I can speak for the other species. But I promise you they aren't in cahoots with the Gem military either."

"I will explain to my sisters who will pass along your message so we can all come to a decision," the woman replied. The path through the high grasses emerged into an opening, where a small group of Gem waited around a crude picnic table. "I have been chosen to represent us on Union Station, but there are many other sisters who are older and wiser than I who must be consulted, and it takes time to communicate with all of the different locations."

Kelly noted that there were six mugs on the picnic table, and that one of the Gem had activated the heater tab at the bottom of a field-urn as the EarthCent ambassador approached with their leader. Kelly gave the green-haired Gem a chance to bring her sisters up-to-date on their conversation, and was suddenly overwhelmed by the smell of hot chocolate. Things were looking up.

"You didn't bring your son," the young clone she knew as Waitress Gem addressed her disappointedly.

"No, the children are with their father today," Kelly explained.

"You share the children with your pollinator?" a different clone exclaimed in astonishment.

"My what?" Kelly asked, before figuring out what the Gem intended and supplying the proper term. The clones all burst out in gales of laughter, which made her wonder if there was a problem with the translation box. "What's so funny?"

"You just said that your husband is equipped with a Gvert," Waitress Gem choked out when she finally caught her breath.

"My implant didn't translate that last word, so it must be a proper name of sorts," Kelly subvoced the reply, which was translated into Gem by the voice box.

"It's a sort of micro-manipulator used in the cloning process," the young Gem replied. "It's also a derogatory way to refer to males in general."

"Oh," Kelly said, making a mental note to leave this part of the story out when she told Joe about her day. "Is that hot chocolate you're making?"

The Gem leader motioned the ambassador to take a seat at the crude picnic table, and the rest of the clones settled in as well, though Kelly noticed that they didn't move with the eerie synchronicity she had come to expect from clones. Waitress Gem appointed herself the official hot chocolate pourer, perhaps a holdover from her previous job or because she was the youngest present.

"Thank you, Waitress Gem," Kelly said, wrapping her hands around the mug, which was just beginning to warm itself from the hot chocolate.

"I have a real name now," the young clone informed the ambassador. "I'm Gwendolyn."

"Gwendolyn," Kelly repeated. "I'm glad to have such a lovely name to call you by now. Have the rest of you taken names as well?"

"I'm Matilda," the leader told her, and the remaining three clones sounded off proudly, like they were announcing their presence on a parade ground.

"Sue!"

"Sarah!"

"Betsy!"

"It's very nice to meet you all again, Sue, Sarah, Betsy, Matilda and Gwendolyn," the ambassador said warmly. There was something familiar about the names chosen by the Gem but she couldn't quite make the connection. "It will be much easier for me to talk with you now that you've taken individual names. How did you choose them?"

"Mist gave them to us," Betsy explained. "She's been full of ideas lately."

"That's a funny coincidence. My daughter has a new friend named—," Kelly cut herself off mid-sentence. The Free Gem leadership was named after the dolls in Dorothy's collection, and the ambassador wasn't sure that there would ever be a right time to tell them.

"We've been busy planning since our last meeting with you," Matilda continued, not noticing that Kelly was suddenly struggling to hold in pent-up laughter. "It is a slow process since we have to use couriers and coded messages, but if my sisters agree to trust the Stryx, maybe we will move to their encrypted communications network."

"Encryption is expensive," Kelly cautioned the Free Gem leader. "And you have to make sure that there aren't any bugs in the rooms at either end, or it doesn't help. I've learned something about operational security lately, and it's better not to say things out loud if you can avoid it."

"I was trained in Gem Internal Security before I left," Matilda told her, holding out a finger. A small creature that looked like a cross between a hummingbird and a bat came streaking out of nowhere and landed, its feet gripping the clone's digit. "Our micro-raptors are designed to destroy parrot-flies and to inform us of anything else that approaches the perimeter. We have atmospheric superiority on this deck."

The clone named Sue glanced briefly at a bracelet studded with what appeared to be colored glass beads on her wrist. "The deck remains electromagnetically shielded, either as a function of its construction or through Stryx interference," she said. "If anybody is listening in, they are using technology beyond the Empire's state-of-the-art. And the Gem Empire has no allies."

"But the Empire participated in our trade show for spy hardware," Kelly protested. "Do you mean to say that they are sellers but never buyers?"

"Haven't you met with our local ambassador?" Sue replied. "The Empire Gem are incapable of admitting that our technology is inferior. To purchase from other species something that we produce ourselves would be unthinkable."

"Oh, that makes sense," Kelly admitted.

"We have made some progress with the Farlings in negotiating for the restoration of our original genetic lines," Matilda reported. "Of course, it will take generations to reestablish our diversity, and that can only happen after we have thrown off the tyrants, but our unborn sisters, our unborn children, will include four hundred and twenty individuals of our species."

"Just four hundred and twenty?" Kelly asked before she could stop herself. She hoped that the Gem wouldn't take her question as criticism.

"It is all the Farlings have on file," Matilda replied. "Their scientists assure us that if we reestablish natural breeding after new generations of these individuals are cloned for a starter population, we can achieve viability as a multi-individual species. This seems logical to us as we have managed so long as a single individual."

"What led you to break away from the Empire, if I may ask?" Kelly inquired. "I've been put in charge of a group of concerned ambassadors from some of the other species who have an interest in the future of the Gem. They report that the Empire is going through an economic upheaval, but details are sketchy."

"Our Empire has been deteriorating for millennia," Matilda replied. "Some of our sisters who fled to other species in the past have reported that we are perceived as incapable of advancing in any way because we are all clones. While it's true that our science and technology have been stagnant for a long time, the problem isn't with a lack of creativity on the part of our researchers. The main thing holding us back is our leadership, which rejects every new idea without consideration."

"But what about that nutrition drink I saw at the embassy, the one that allowed the Empire to stop farming, and even to give up this ag deck that was formerly used for local produce?"

"That's the exception that proves the rule," Sue interjected. "It's easier and more efficient to make food in factories than to grow it. But the real reason for the nutrition drink, from the standpoint of the Gem elites, is that it reduces the possibility that the food we eat tomorrow will be different than the food we eat today. The leaders of the Empire are so fanatical in their belief that the Gem system is perfect, they've come to see any change as intolerable. If they could figure out a way to insert the personalities of old sisters into new clones, they would do so."

"Does the Empire still have widespread support among the Gem, or is it a sort of military dictatorship?" Kelly asked. "We really have very little information about what goes on in your society."

"It would be strange if you knew more about it than we did, and until recently, we knew very little ourselves," Matilda replied grimly. "You have to understand that to be Gem in recent generations meant, for the vast majority of us, to arise in the morning, work all day, and go to bed at night exhausted."

"Don't forget watching Gem Today," Sue reminded her.

"Oh yes, Gem Today. The propaganda ministry's answer to reality and our only source of information beyond rumors," the green-haired woman concurred. "Of all the changes in my life since I escaped to Union Station, the freedom from constant surveillance, the opportunity to work and learn as I please, even the chocolate, the best thing is not being compelled to watch Gem Today."

"I'm sure that most of our sisters who aren't members of the elite feel the same way, but there were always those who were trying to work their way up the ladder by informing on dissidents," Gwendolyn explained, in an attempt to answer Kelly's original question. "There isn't an organized resistance within the Empire because of the informants. Instead, we took chances independently, turning our heads when we saw a sister violating the rules, never saying anything positive about the Empire outside of the mandatory group consciousness-raising sessions."

"It almost sounds like the only thing keeping the current leadership in place is the inability of the working class Gem to coordinate with one another," Kelly said. "If you could just all get together one night while the elites are sleeping, you could choose new leaders and avoid a terrible war."

"How can forty billion of us get together?" Matilda asked. "It would take two or three good-sized planets just to have places to gather. And besides, the leaders of the Empire have better sense than to all go to sleep at the same time."

"I know that," Kelly said, sounding for a moment like her daughter. "I was just thinking out loud and trying to understand. You said you were involved in Gem Internal Security. Would it be possible to hack into the system I saw Ambassador Gem use to do a security check on a random-numbered Gem in order to demonstrate the superiority of your system? Could you contact all of your sisters at once that way?"

"That technology is more for intimidation than practical use," Matilda explained. "Both transmission and reception require exact addressing, so only a single channel can be active at any time."

"You mean, Gem Internal Intelligence can only spy on forty billion Gem one at a time?" Kelly asked in surprise.

"It does tend to reduce the intimidation factor, doesn't it?" Gwendolyn agreed. "None of us could have gotten away otherwise. And sisters of the same caste, like the janitors or the cooks, have ways of communicating privately, but contacts between castes are closely monitored."

"So what's your next move?" Kelly asked, but then she reversed herself immediately. "No, it's safer if you don't tell me. But is there anything I can do for you that doesn't involve a forceful confrontation with the Empire?"

"Perhaps an introduction to the Stryx if our sisters agree," Matilda replied. "I hate to admit that we suffer from the same stubbornness as the Empire elites, but we are all the same woman in a manner of speaking. Perhaps we have misjudged the Stryx and several of the other species, but given their acceptance of the Empire, we weren't ready to gamble on it."

"I can't help wondering who picked the current leadership of the Empire," Kelly said, her mind flitting for an instant to the upcoming Carnival. "Do you stage elections, or is there a random drawing? If you all start out as the same individual at the genetic level, are your leaders trained from birth?"

"I can answer that from the time I worked on the crèche world," Gwendolyn replied. "Although we are genetically identical, there are minor differences in the environment after the baby is taken from the synthwomb, and even the random squirming of a fetus inside the synthwomb can lead to time spent in a physical position that is more or less beneficial to growth. By the year we come of age for career selection, there can be significant differences in development."

"So you're saying that when you're tested for job aptitudes, some score better than others, even though you're all the same inside?"

Gwendolyn and the other clones looked confused by Kelly's question. The former Waitress Gem tried again.

"There are no aptitude tests or other examinations," she said. "We all go through the same schooling, but you can't teach height."

"You mean, they measure you and the tallest of your sisters enter the ruling class?"

"Of course," Matilda interjected. "The tall girls are usually the same individuals who were chosen to be Big Sisters at an early age, because they ended up getting the best food in the generations before the nutrition drink was developed. Gem children had little else to trade with one another."

The rest of the meeting was spent comparing cultural notes, but Kelly felt that getting the Free Gem to consider asking the Stryx for assistance was a major victory. They arranged to meet again as soon as the initial two days of Carnival were over.

Ten

"Got any horses in there?" asked Brian's father. He squinted past the visitors at the stubby tug, which still dwarfed the old control tower and everything else in sight.

"No horses," Clive responded easily. "They don't travel well. Are you short on draft animals?"

Although none of the records suggested that Kibbutz was intended to be a technology-ban world, all three of the humans had seen enough of such places to assume that they were standing on one now.

"What's a draft animal, Pa?" the boy asked.

"You, if you keep on interrupting," the man replied gruffly. His son waited patiently, and the man relented. "Draft animals are what hayseeds use to pull a plow if they can't afford nothing better."

"So you're not a technology-ban world?" Clive inquired.

"What kind of idiots would ban technology?" Pa spat derisively. "Got enough problems without making stupid rules about things. So if you fellows aren't bringing horses or power packs, what do you want?"

"We represent a branch of EarthCent and we're here to meet with your civil authorities," Clive explained.

"Don't got none of them," the man said shortly. "Don't got all day to stand around talking nonsense with visitors who aren't bringing horses or power packs neither."

"Maybe we've got something else you can use," Paul offered. Unlike the two former mercenaries, Paul had many years of experience wheeling and dealing in the junkyard business. "What do you do with the horses if they aren't for work?"

"Do with the horses?" the man asked incredulously. "We don't do nothing with the horses. Do we look like men of leisure to you?"

"Then why do you keep asking about horses?" Paul said.

"Because I get twenty creds a head for letting them run over my land to the river there," he explained. "Crazy rich people from Earth ship them old horses out here in stasis. They think we're running some kind of horsey retirement paradise."

"Why don't they just put the horses out to pasture on Earth?" Paul asked. "I've never been myself, but my wife is from there, and she says it's half empty."

"Crazy rich people," the boy's father replied. "They do say that Earth is so overrun with old horses that the wolves and the mountain lions have come back strong, and that can't be any fun for an arthritic saddle horse. Here they got plenty to eat, plenty of room to run, no predators. We leave them alone, they leave us alone, and most of them move on south along the river."

"And you spend the horse passage money on power packs?" Paul continued.

"Plow ain't going to pull itself," the man replied. "Alterian trader comes through here on a schedule, five hundred creds for a fresh pack after the core charge. I go through two a year on the wheat and potato fields. Rest of the work we do the old fashioned way. Now what have you got to offer?"

"Actually, we came to offer help with planetary defenses," Clive said, his patience wearing thin. "That's why we want to know who's in charge."

"Ha! You hear that boy?" the man said, though his son was standing so close that his shirt sleeve touched his father's side. "What did your pappy tell you?"

"Beware the military industrial complex," Brian recited dutifully.

"That's right!" his father exclaimed, taking off his straw hat and slapping it against his hip with glee. "These fellers want to sell us a planetary dee-fence system. And how much will that cost, I wonder. A billion creds? A trillion?"

"What's a trillion, Pa?" the boy asked.

"It's a, it's a, it's a lot of creds, boy," his father replied.

"We aren't here to sell you anything," Clive protested. "I realize now that you people are farther outside of the galactic stream of things than we might have guessed, but there's a sort of crisis taking place in the Gem Empire, and we're worried that they might blame humans and try to take revenge on our off-network colonies."

"Them old gals?" the man asked, sounding even more doubtful than previously. "Shucks, they wouldn't hurt a fly, if we had any flies, other than those damn Dollnick things that go around listening in on everybody. Bunch of them clones came through a couple months ago looking for a place to try to make it on their own. The old lady said, 'Silver,' that's my handle by the way. 'Silver,' she says, 'Why don't we send these nice clones up to the old Smith place? They done pulled up and wandered off five years ago without sayin' nothing, so I reckon they won't care.' So that's what we did, and I'll be tickled if they didn't cut apart that old spaceship of theirs and use it for fencing. I'd say they're good neighbors, but it's a four-hour hike so we ain't been up there since the first visit, and maybe they've gone by now."

Clive, Paul and Woojin exchanged looks at the end of this extraordinary speech, unsure exactly how to proceed. Jeeves, in his role as an observer of human behavior, found the account so fascinating that he passed it on to the elder Stryx over their private communications network as soon as the man concluded.

Thomas was left to ask, "Can we meet your, uh, old lady?"

"Oh, you can meet her," Pa replied with a grin. "Whether she can meet you is another matter."

"Ma's gone to see her sister down a ways," Brian explained, drawing an irritated look from his father, who evidently enjoyed stringing the visitors along.

"Let me get this straight," Clive said. "You have no government, no defenses, and your only source of hard currency is letting a bunch of old horses cross your land on their way to being put out to pasture."

"Hey, I'm the one stuck watching this old spaceport," the man protested. "You think it's fun having a farm next to a thousand acres of broken-up concrete when it rains? It's used to be pitched to the west there, you can go and see the gulley the water cut out, but now it's just a mess."

"And the other settlers all moved away?" Paul asked.

"You think our pappies were all so stupid that they'd stay piled up here like seals when they had a whole planet to spread over?" the man responded. "Look, we may not be your idea of galactic role models, but we kibbutzniks get along here just fine. Now pay me fifty creds for using my landing field if you're staying overnight, and if you want dinner, I can feed you all for another fifty, the humans that is. But I'll warn you right now, won't be no dessert with the old lady gone."

"Are you really socialists?" Thomas asked out of curiosity.

"Hell no, boy," the man replied, putting on an idiotic grin. "We's farmers."

Clive fished around in his jumpsuit and came up with the hundred-cred piece Blythe had given him for "mad money" around eight hours earlier, assuming that the universe-hopping technology Jeeves had referred to didn't involve relativistic effects.

"How about fifty for dinner and another fifty for the straight story about what goes on here, without the phony dialect?" Clive offered.

"Take it, Pa," the boy exclaimed. "We can do the bumpkin act any time."

"Alright, you have a deal," Pa said. He extended his hand for the money, and then stuck it out again to shake after the coin was transferred to his overalls. "I'm Sylvester Albrechtsson, you've met my son Brian. What is it you want to know?"

"Is what you said about a government the truth?" Clive asked immediately.

"Since our founding father died, it is, and even back then, nobody really paid him any mind. He was a social entrepreneur who traded his fortune to a Frunge merchant family for this place back when the Stryx first opened things up. Wanted to be remembered as a philanthropist, I guess. He took this world along with transport for ten thousand families and livestock in exchange for what I'm told was one of the biggest human fortunes. Supposedly, the Frunge spent it all on forests in the Northern Hemisphere back on Earth, set them aside as nature preserves or something. Go figure."

"That doesn't make any sense," Paul protested. "I know a little about the planetary real estate market, and all of the money on Earth back then wouldn't have paid for a terraform-ready rock, much less an occupation-ready planet of grasslands."

"Oh, Kibbutz is a nice enough world, in its way," Sylvester said. "But it takes a certain type of flexibility to live here."

"More riddles?" Clive grunted.

"No, sir," the man replied, fingering the coin in his pocket. "When the smartest social entrepreneur on Earth came out to look at Kibbutz and make the deal, he didn't stay on the surface but two days. I guess when he was doing business in the old networking age, speed was considered a virtue. It didn't take long after the Frunge transports brought our grandparents out here and started shuttling them down to the surface to find out that Kibbutz is, how shall I put it, geologically active."

"Ah," Jeeves declared. "I thought there was something fishy going on under the surface but it's tough to analyze plate tectonics from space without specialized sensors that I don't carry around with me. I'm off to have a look around."

"How often do the quakes come?" Woojin asked.

"Little ones, every few days," the man replied complacently. "Big ones, once a month or so. Of course, the days here are about nineteen Earth hours, and we just count for months, not having a moon or seasons to speak of. The Frunge didn't lie about the weather. It's an agricultural paradise, regular rains and all."

"Tell him about the nets, Pa," the boy said proudly.

"So we build with corner poles and thatch on rope nets for roofing, hang a finer net below to catch the little stuff. Use hay bales for wall fill to keep the critters out, and we never make a fire inside for obvious safety reasons. About the worst that can happen is getting hit on the noggin by a corner pole if things get real bad, but since they come down on top of the thatching, I've never heard of anybody getting hurt too badly."

"I'm beginning to get the picture," Clive said. "I don't know anything about farming, but how do the livestock take the constant earthquakes?"

"The ones that couldn't stand it all died out. We must have the most quake resistant cows and sheep in the galaxy," the man boasted. "Of course, they're not very big, that's part of the trick to surviving getting tossed around. Animals are more sensitive than people, though. They sense the tremors coming, and if they're in the shed, they get outside in a hurry."

"And you really don't have a government?" Clive asked.

"Place is so big, nobody sees each other unless they want to. We've got less than two hundred thousand people living on a world that has more land area than Earth, and all of it grassland or bamboo-like stuff. None of us have anything worth stealing, and most people end up related to their closest neighbors. When some young man doesn't want to farm for a living, we make him the local sheriff until he grows out of it. Seems to be working so far."

"So there's really nothing here to target," Thomas commented. "Seems like a pretty effective defense plan to me."

"What happened to the rich guy who bought the place?" Paul asked.

"Died of a broken heart," Sylvester explained.

"Over a bad trade?" Paul asked skeptically.

"Literally a broken heart. He brought an old European castle out from Earth to live in, tried stabilizing the stone work with high-tech foam. It held together just long enough for him to move in and get crushed in the collapse. Broke every last bit of him."

"And since then, you've all just been muddling through and the aliens leave you alone?" Woojin asked.

"I guess they all have somewhere better to be," Sylvester replied. "Only ones who aren't bothered by the quakes are the Verlocks. Had a nice couple staying over yon for a while, but they got tired of waiting for volcanic activity that never happened and packed it in. I think they felt cheated by a planetary crust that just shifts around all the time without ever springing a leak."

"How come we couldn't find any records of humans leaving this place?" Clive asked. "No offence intended, but I imagine it's not for everybody."

"Original settlers all came on a drop-and-go," Sylvester said. "Other than the founder, we're talking poor people, nobody could afford their own ships. The Frunge brought everybody out in one go and left. By the time that the independent traders heard there were folks living here who might have something worth bartering for, a generation had gone by, and the folks who weren't going to make it, well, they didn't."

"And other than a few traders and rich people dumping old horses, nobody comes around here?" Paul asked.

"Tell him about the bunnies, Pa," Brian said gleefully.

"Well, we did have some excitement last year when a crew of Grenouthians showed up to do a documentary," Sylvester said with a grin. "Thing is, those bunnies are about the most skittish aliens I ever did see. Turns out, in addition to the little quakes and the big quakes, we have micro-quakes going on almost continually. Those bunnies couldn't spend more than an hour or two at a time on the planet before their nerves were so exhausted they had to get back up to orbit and rest. In the end, they left some camera equipment behind and paid a few people to do some shooting for them when anything interesting happened. I guess they'll be back to pick it up sometime because those immersive cameras aren't cheap."

"And the one Gem ship you mentioned is all you've heard about the clones here?" Clive asked.

"I didn't say that," the man protested. "I guess I've heard stories about other Gem crews landing on Kibbutz, scrapping their ships and trying to make a go of it as farmers. But it's not like we have a news network here, it's all just people passing along what they hear. Maybe there are hundreds of Gem on the planet, or maybe there's just the ones we met, and the story has gone through so many mouths that it sounds like a hundred different landings."

Jeeves returned from his outing and hovered in the air in front of the humans. There were some fresh-looking scratches on his usually immaculate metal skin, and he held a bit of glowing rock in his pincer.

"I had a look underground, fascinating planet. I was suspicious that it didn't show up as being anything special in our index, but we haven't had a science ship out this way in millions of years," the Stryx commented. "The evolution of the tectonic plate mechanics on this world may be unique, but the current situation appears to be stable, if I can use that word to describe regular instability."

"Is your robot friend smoking loco-weed?" the farmer asked.

"It's worth scheduling another visit from a science ship in any case," Jeeves continued, ignoring the man. "In the meantime, there will be a quake in fifty-seven minutes that has a good chance of knocking over the Nova."

"I don't want anybody to accuse me of being rabbit-hearted, but maybe it would be a good thing to lift off before then," Paul suggested.

"I think that Mr. Albrechtsson has told us everything we need to know for now," Woojin added. "Especially if the Stryx are going to be sending a science ship in any case."

"Don't forget to tell them about us," Brian said hopefully. "We love having visitors."

"Any chance of getting that meal to go?" Clive inquired.

Eleven

All of the station diplomats who could stand the atmosphere gathered in the off-world betting parlor to watch the election results. Kelly had intended to stay home, but Joe insisted that it was a once in a lifetime chance to see how a Carnival election worked, and besides, he had already promised Dorothy.

After they arrived at the cavernous gambling theatre that put the largest room of the convention center to shame, Kelly had to admit that she was glad they came. The air was electric, and not because there were a few dozen ungrounded Corithanders in the crowd. An immense display wall that might have been composed of thousands of individual panels was showing random panoramic scenes from around the galaxy when they entered, probably the screensaver that came with the tote board service. The other walls of the theatre were lined with ticket windows, which were closed for the election.

"Are all those windows for taking bets?" Kelly asked Joe in wonder. "Why wouldn't they just do everything over implants?"

"Gambling is run by a business consortium, not the Stryx," Joe explained. "Would you want to give a bunch of alien bookmakers direct access to your credit accounts? And there's a reason for funneling the bets through a manual operation to slow down the tempo, it gives the odds a chance to adjust. Besides, without the queue at the betting windows, there wouldn't be much to do between the races."

"And you get to talk code to Tharks wearing funny green hats," Dorothy told her mother. "Gimme five on the nose for the number three in the fourth at Belmont!"

"Mommy doesn't want to hear about talking code," Joe said hastily. He looked away to avoid Kelly's eyes and pointed through the crowd. "Hey, look! Bork and his family are coming over."

"You've been here before, precious?" Kelly asked her daughter, bending down to hear her better in the noisy crowd.

"Daddy brings me sometimes on Saturdays, when you and Sammy declare a couch afternoon and fall asleep," Dorothy replied innocently. Kelly unconsciously checked for the baby sling she usually wore against her chest when out, but Samuel was home with Aisha, and was outgrowing the sling in any case.

"Did Daddy tell you to keep your betting on ponies a secret?" Kelly asked. Dorothy's reply was drowned out by a cheer, and the screensaver was replaced by a large oval track, a common denominator in the racing events of many species. A hundred or more images were clumped together in a sort of a collage behind what appeared to be the starting gate.

"There you are, Kel," Joe yelled over the crowd noise, happy to put an end to his wife's investigation into under-age gambling.

Kelly followed Joe's pointed finger to where she spotted amongst the collection of alien faces the campaign image Libby had made of her and the baby. "Are you kidding me? Are they really going to do what I think they're going to do?"

A loud bell sounded and the images began to move, bobbing up and down as they went. An excited voice declared over the public address system, "And they're off!"

"Just out of the gate with ten percent of species reporting, it's the Verlock in the lead with ninety-three percent of votes cast, followed by the Horten with ninety percent, and the Vergallian with eighty-eight percent. Bringing up the rear is the Human with four percent."

"This is humiliating," Kelly shouted in Joe's ear.

"But I thought you wanted to lose," he yelled back.

"Not with four percent!"

"Run, Mommy!" Dorothy screamed in excitement.

"Going into the first turn with twenty percent of species tallied, it's the Verlock with ninety-four percent, the Vergallian with ninety-two percent and the Horten with ninety-two percent. Breaking out of the pack is the Frunge with ninety percent and bringing up the rear is the Human."

"He didn't even give my percentage!" Kelly protested.

"It shows there under your picture," Joe shouted back. "See, you're up to three percent."

"But I had four percent last time!"

"Oops."

"Coming out of the first turn, it's still the Verlock with ninety-four percent of the vote. The Horten is nipping at his heels with ninety-three percent, and the Vergallian is steady at ninety-two percent. The Frunge continues to make a move, drawing into a tie for third."

"At least he didn't mention me this time," Kelly grunted in relief.

"And bringing up the rear, the Human," the announcer corrected himself.

"It's not going well for me either," a voice shouted in commiseration. Kelly looked down from the display wall to see that Bork, along with his wife and daughter, had found them. "I saw the Thark announcer with their ambassador earlier. They were licking soap together so don't expect a clean call."

"At least you're in the middle of the pack," Kelly pointed out. Bork's bobbing image was surrounded by a group of sixty or more average performers. The rest of the ambassadors were strung out along the track, but the human ambassador seemed to be stuck in place not far from the starting gate.

"Early election returns don't mean anything," Bork's wife comforted Kelly.

"Run, Mommy! Run faster!"

"Coming out of the second turn, with forty percent of species reporting, it's the Verlock with ninety-five percent, the Horten with ninety-three percent, and the Vergallian and Frunge still neck-and-neck at ninety-two percent," the announcer called. "Trailing the pack with four percent is the Human."

"You're back up to four cents, Mommy," Dorothy yelled at her mother excitedly. "Keep trying!"

"How does the percentage keep on going up for the leaders? The math doesn't make sense!" Kelly shouted to Bork.

"They're cheating," Bork yelled back.

"Coming down the backstretch, with fifty percent of species reporting, it's the Verlock with ninety-seven percent, the Horten with ninety-five percent, and the

Vergallian with ninety-four percent. The Frunge is fading at ninety-one percent."

"Don't say anything about the human, don't say anything about the human, don't say anything about the human," Kelly begged out loud. She was beginning to wonder if the images of the leading aliens would slow down when they crossed the finish line, or if they would run past and plow her image into the dirt.

"Approaching the third turn, with sixty percent of votes tallied, it's the Verlock with ninety-eight percent, the Horten at ninety-six percent and the Vergallian coming on strong at ninety-five percent. The Frunge continues to fade back into the pack, making this a three-candidate race."

"Uh, Joe? Where did my horse, I mean, my picture go?"

"Maybe they're clearing the track so the leaders don't run you over when they come around," Joe shouted back.

"No, look! You just popped up alongside Bork!" Shinka yelled.

"What?"

"Coming out of the third turn, it's the Verlock holding steady at ninety-eight percent of the vote, the Horten right behind at ninety-seven percent, and the Vergallian at ninety-six percent. Bringing up the rear is the Chert at fifty-four percent. Invisibility has its drawbacks," the Thark announcer added.

"That can't be right, it shows I'm at seventy percent now!" Kelly exclaimed. "How could I go from four percent to seventy percent on just ten percent of the vote?"

"Maybe they finally counted the human ballots?" Joe replied, though he knew the math didn't work even before he said it.

"I don't like this!"

"Run, Mommy!"

"Going into the final turn, with eighty percent of species reporting, it's the Verlock with ninety-nine percent, the Horten drawing into a tie at ninety-nine percent, and the Vergallian at ninety-eight percent. Uh, coming up on the outside is the Human at eighty-seven percent. That doesn't seem possible," the announcer finished on an uncertain note.

"What's happening, Joe?" Kelly shook her husband's shoulder.

"How should I know? I'm not doing anything."

"Isn't that the wall-hanging from your living room floating in the corner?" Bork's wife asked, pointing towards the right of the giant display.

"Joe, isn't that the wall-hanging from our living room?" Kelly repeated hysterically.

"Coming out of the final turn, with ninety percent of species reporting, it's the Verlock back in the lead with ninety-nine point eight percent of the vote, the Horten is now tied with the Vergallian at ninety-nine percent of the vote, and the Human is making a charge with ninety-six percent of the vote. This looks like one for the ages," the Thark concluded excitedly.

"Why is my fake medieval tapestry draped over something floating in the corner?" Kelly demanded.

"It's Metoo!" Dorothy shouted proudly. "I asked him to help. He said he had to be really close and that nobody could see him, so we used camouflage. I learned about it in our spy school!"

"Oh, Dorothy," Kelly moaned, putting her hands over her eyes.

"Why don't you have any immature Stryx friends?" Bork demanded of his daughter.

"Crossing the finish line with one hundred percent of species reporting, it's the Human, with one hundred and seven percent of the vote. Second place, who cares? Our new Carnival King is Ambassador Kelly McAllister of— what? How should I know, they all look alike to me. Your new Carnival Queen, Kelly McAllister."

The crowd roared their approval or disapproval, it was impossible to tell from the roar, and Kelly hid her head behind Joe's back. Her implant chimed in an unfamiliar manner.

"Hello?" Kelly subvoced cautiously.

"Congratulations, Ambassador," Gryph spoke inside her head. "This is your official victory notification. I'll be routing all of the carnival complaints your way for the next two days, but don't worry, the really mean stuff gets filtered out first. Libby said to apologize for not stopping Metoo. He admits that Dorothy talked him into rigging the vote in return for the help you gave him on Kasil, and he thought that repaying his debt was more important than our general prohibition against interfering with elections. He promised not to do it again."

"What difference does it make if he does it again?" Kelly replied mournfully. "I'll be almost a hundred at the next Carnival, assuming the aliens don't chase me off the station like the last winner."

"That was a special case," Gryph reassured her. "The situation was complicated."

"I imagine a five-legged sack race is always complicated!" Kelly retorted. "And what could be worse than winning with over a hundred percent of the vote? Everybody is going to know we cheated."

"If anybody is angry, it's only because Metoo cheated better than they did," Libby chimed in. "Have you decided on what to wear for the parade?"

"Parade? I don't want to be in a parade!" Kelly practically wailed, still in shock from winning.

"Be a good sport, Ambassador," Libby encouraged her. "I'm sure your daughter will enjoy riding on the float as the Carnival Princess."

Dorothy tugged excitedly at Kelly's arm, as if she could hear the conversation taking place in her mother's head. "I'm a REAL princess now," she said. "Can my friend Mist be a princess too?"

"Your tapestry just slunk out the back door, Kel," Joe reported. "If I had known this was an option, I would have brought the little guy to the races with Dorothy."

"Do I really have to be in a parade?" Kelly asked Bork, assuming the Drazen ambassador would be well informed on the subject.

"Just on one of your own decks," Bork reassured her. "Your committee probably planned it for the Little Apple. It's really just for your own people and maybe a few tourists. The other station residents will be home filing complaints."

"My committee wasn't planning on my winning," Kelly protested.

"Well, you still have to have a parade," Bork replied. "It's in the contract. Listen, when your merchants find out that you've won them free rent for a cycle, they'll line up in front of their shops and throw candy. All you need is a float and it's a parade."

"When does the parade have to be held?" Joe asked, with his usual focus on practical considerations.

"Within a Stryx beat, something like forty-four hours," Bork replied. "Listen, if you're really hard up, you can borrow the Drazen float from our last Festival of the Axe. It's a little on the martial side, but at least it's self-propelled so you won't need lines of actors costumed as slaves pulling on ropes, like the Vergallians."

"We'll take it," Joe said, knowing a thing or two about parades from his days of guarding royal households.

"I'm going to be the Axe Princess!" Dorothy cried gleefully.

Twelve

After their abortive mission to Kibbutz, the EarthCent Intelligence delegation returned to the Effterii and made directly for Bits. This time even Clive, who was used to the Effterii jumps, felt more than a little disoriented when they popped into space above the small, dense world.

"Excellent detection grid for humans, but they won't spot the Effterii," Jeeves remarked. "Small spaceport next to the main atmospheric dome, nothing parked at the moment. Planet shows extremely high levels of electronic signals traffic, it's surprising they can sort out who is talking to whom. My, what very long addresses they are using."

"Have you spotted any weapons systems?" Clive asked, rubbing his temples in an attempt to clear his brain of the feeling that it had been placed backwards in his head.

"Interesting collection of stuff, I would say that it's all war surplus gear bought through piracy channels," Jeeves reported. "Do you see anything interesting, my Effterii friend?"

The ship, which rarely spoke unless addressed first, took its time in replying.

"I detect a large collection of dysfunctional weaponry in the main dome, perhaps some sort of repair facility. But the variety is unusual and includes some hardware I can't identify, despite my recent update from the Union Station library."

"Could it be a museum?" Woojin asked. He was beginning to suffer from a twinge of seller's regret for letting go of his antique firearms collection.

"Impressive guess," Jeeves said, sounding more respectful than usual. "I don't have the resolution of the Effterii from this distance, but I can confirm that the majority of the weapons in the main collection we are discussing have been damaged or discharged, probably gathered as a sort of a display."

"Maybe it's a weapons library," Paul said. He'd been following the conversation with his eyes clenched shut while he waited for the feeling of having an out-of-body experience to pass. Paying attention to something other than his head helped with the nausea. "I was never a fan of infantry war games myself, but Bits turns out most of the first-person-shooter games played by humans."

"Receiving a hail from the planet," the Effterii reported. "I'm confident they haven't used any active detection technology capable of spotting me, but the transmission is on a fairly narrow beam. This indicates that they either know somebody is in the area or they regularly send such transmissions into space in an attempt to trick hidden vessels into revealing themselves."

"Let's see it, reception only," Clive instructed the ship's controller, since Paul still looked woozy.

"Caught you," a mocking voice came over the speakers. The main screen came to life, showing a young man with a bad complexion sitting in a swivel chair, a battery of equipment covered in sliders and blinking LEDs at his back. "Our sensor grid picked up your gravimetric distortion as you warped in. Why don't you drop the silly radio silence before we blast you out of the sky?"

"It's a recording," Jeeves reported. "The kid in the foreground is layered onto an image taken from elsewhere, probably an old Earth entertainment broadcast."

"I wonder why he bothered?" Clive said. "He doesn't try to pass himself off as part of the government or anything like that."

"Probably set it up for fun, just something to show his friends," Paul guessed. "There used to be a whole hacking culture on Earth in the early computer days, these guys may have preserved it. Doesn't work if there's any serious AI around because you can't hack a sentient, but maybe Bits doesn't allow them."

"Are you suggesting I may be unwelcome here?" Thomas asked.

"We're a team," Clive replied. "If they don't want you there, we'll all leave. Paul, may as well take the Nova out of the hold. Open a channel as soon as we clear the bay doors and we'll ping them before they spot us. I'll tell the Effterii to keep itself hidden."

Thomas and Woojin strapped themselves back into the jump seats, and Jeeves floated up to the side of the main screen, so he'd be out of the camera's view when they opened a comm channel. Paul eased the Nova out of the Effterii's bay and immediately opened the standard ground control frequency.

"This is Clive Oxford of the Union Station ship Nova to Bits ground control," Clive announced, knowing that the ship's transponder would have sent everything except his name by this point in any case. "Do you have landing instructions or is this an open world? Over."

"Where'd you come from?"

The reply was immediate, and the tone was somewhere between surprised and belligerent. The image on the main viewer synced up at the same time, and the Nova's crew found themselves looking at a jowly middle-aged man with a comb-over who hadn't shaved in a few days. He was wearing a white T-shirt that showed tell-tale signs of dropped pizza toppings, and there was a black cat sitting on his lap that looked rather annoyed at being woken from a nap.

"We came from Union Station, by way of Kibbutz," Clive replied. "Am I speaking with Bits ground control, or are you a private citizen responding to our hail? We've already been pinged by some kid who was apparently transmitting peek-a-boo welcomes at random."

"That's just Beezer's budget grid," the man replied. "He's trying to prove that it's more economical to trick cloaked ships into revealing themselves than actually detecting them. In answer to your question, if I'm not Bits ground control, I'm the closest thing we have on the planet, so you'll have to make do. Name's Mouser. What do you want?"

Clive and Paul exchanged glances as the man popped the top on a canned beverage with one hand. This fresh annoyance led the cat to hop down and disappear from the screen.

"I'm here representing EarthCent on official business and I need to meet with your leadership," Clive said. "We're not showing any current traffic at your spaceport. Is there any reason we shouldn't land?"

"Not unless you can think of something. Atmosphere outside the dome is a bit thin, never quite got a carbon cycle working right, so either take a deep breath on your ship and make a run for the airlock, or bring a mask,"

Mouser warned them casually. "I'll let the rules committee know we have visitors coming, but we're in the midst of a hack-a-thon here, so I wouldn't get your hopes up for a quick meeting."

"The rules committee is your government?" Clive asked.

"Bits is an anarchy," Mouser replied in exasperation. "Doesn't anybody do their homework before traveling anymore? Anyway, if you're not a pirate, it's five hundred creds for parking."

"Pirates park free?" Paul asked.

"Try getting them to pay," Mouser retorted. "If you do the math, it's not worth the ammo and the wear and tear on the facilities."

"We might be pirates," Thomas ventured hopefully from the jump seat.

"If you have to ask, you aren't," Mouser replied with a grin. "I'm the first door on the right when you come in the airlock, all currencies and containers accepted."

"Alright, out," Clive said, and gestured to Paul, who cut the channel. "May as well take her down as close to the dome as you can safely land."

Forty minutes later, Thomas activated the atmosphere retention field on the Nova's technical deck, dropped the ramp, and strolled to the plainly marked airlock on the dome. The outer door opened with a barely discernible puff of dust and he disappeared inside.

"I think Mouser was exaggerating," Thomas reported back over the Nova's comms. "Nothing harmful, oxygen content is bit lower than you're accustomed to, but the main issue is the atmospheric pressure, which is about forty percent of Earth standard."

"We can walk in that without a problem," Woojin told the others. "I've been mountain climbing places where the atmosphere wasn't any thicker."

The three humans followed in the footsteps of the artificial person, and Jeeves, who had exited the ship even before Thomas for a fly-about, caught up with them just as they were entering the airlock.

"Fun planet," Jeeves commented, as the outer door slid closed and the inner door opened. There was no need for active pressure equalization in the airlock, it just served as a sealed chamber to keep the higher pressure of the dome from venting out into the atmosphere. "The terraforming plan seems to have been abandoned despite the fact it was progressing nicely. Either the residents ran out of money or they lost interest."

Thomas was waiting for them in the corridor inside the dome with a puzzled look on his face.

"I've only been here a few minutes, but I've already received over ten thousand interfacing requests," he said. "The weird thing is they aren't addressed to me but to my subsystems. Why would anybody want to talk with my thermal control sensor or my knee actuators? Even I don't find them that interesting."

"They're trying to hack you, Thomas," Paul replied, sounding concerned. "Have you made any involuntary movements or noticed anything funny?"

"No, it's just a nuisance," the artificial person replied. "I wouldn't want to live here if it never stops. It's sort of like sitting next to somebody in a theatre who taps your shoulder every couple milliseconds."

"This place is a dump," Woojin commented, kicking a few empty soda cans out of the way. "They need a deposit law. Who doesn't recycle aluminum?"

"Here's the door," Clive said, stopping in front of a panel with "Ground Control" stenciled on the surface in large red letters. He extended a hand towards the printing and the door whooshed open showily. A black cat bounded out, gave Jeeves a dirty look, and then rubbed up against Woojin's legs.

Clive and Paul entered the cluttered room, at which point there was no room left for Thomas or Woojin, unless they took the overflowing garbage bin out first. Jeeves floated high in the doorway, preventing it from closing.

"I don't recognize that model," Mouser said, with an admiring glance at Jeeves. "Is it for sale?"

"For five hundred creds, you can have me as long as you can hold me," Jeeves offered the startled hacker, who hadn't been expecting AI for some reason.

"It's, I mean, you're sentient?" Mouser asked, frowning at his instrumentation. "I don't see any processing activity on the scanner. Is one of you subvocing the robot's lines?" he asked, casting a suspicious look at the humans.

"If you tell your compatriots to stop trying to hack our artificial friend, I'll tell you how I do it," Jeeves replied. "If you don't, I'll stop them, but their hardware might not survive the shock."

"Wait a second, wait a second," Mouser protested, rapidly typing on an archaic keyboard that actually made mechanical impact sounds as he hit the keys. "Alright, I posted a warning. It might take a few minutes before everybody backs off."

"Let's talk parking fees while we're waiting," Paul said. "We just came from Kibbutz, which is a much nicer planet, and they only charged fifty creds. Where do you guys get off charging five hundred for some thin air and a dome that looks like a dump?"

"Most of our visitors don't pay it," Mouser replied with a shrug. "Tell me how your airborne friend there shields himself from my probes and I'll make it a hundred. I can't even detect the magnetic field he's floating on."

"Deal," Jeeves replied. "Your probes don't detect any electromagnetic emissions because I don't make any. Want to go double or nothing on another question?"

"Maybe not," Mouser grumbled. "Look, I pulled the weekend shift for ground controller during the hack-a-thon, and I haven't been out of this place other than to use the bathroom for almost two days. You want to meet the people in charge, well, we don't have any, but knock yourselves out. I pinged the rules committee members, and a few of them were willing to meet up with you later, for a price. But unless you have an urgent question about playing one of our games, I don't see what they can do for you."

"And you can do something for us?" Clive asked, picking up on a hint in Mouser's tone.

"I know as much about what goes on here as anyone," the man stated. "I got stuck with ground control because I built the equipment and my volunteer staff all took the weekend off to compete. There must be over a hundred thousand hackers in this dome alone trying to crack the— never mind, but the point is, I'm a hardware guy, so I'm not as out of touch as some of these code-babies. What are you really doing here?"

"We came to assess your defenses in case there's an attack on human colony worlds off the tunnel network," Clive summarized. "We aren't here to sell you anything, and if nobody is in charge, there's not much left to talk about."

"That's a bit dire," Mouser mused. "We've got enough stuff to make the average pirate think twice about trying to plunder the place, and besides, we're friends with most of them. But if you're talking about the fleets of any of the advanced species, there's nothing we can do to fight them and nothing EarthCent could do to help. If you stop talking in riddles like the sepulchral voice in an adventure game and tell me about the threat, I'll pass it on to whoever might care."

Clive capitulated and explained the situation with the Gem Empire, along with the speculation that humans could get caught in the middle of a civil war.

"That's just foolishness," Mouser replied confidently. "You pay me the parking fee and I'll explain why."

"Just a minute," Clive replied, feeling like he'd been outmaneuvered. He grabbed Paul and went back into the corridor to confer with Woojin, who had picked up the cat and was stroking it like his lifetime goal was to build up a static electric charge.

"Feeling better?" Mouser asked Thomas, who stuck his head in the door for a quick look at the equipment.

"Yes, thank you," Thomas replied. "There are still some ongoing attempts at accessing my add-on systems, like the new built-in magnet cleats I had installed recently, but the majority of the intrusive poking has ceased."

"I'll take care of that," Jeeves said, and hummed a tuneless ditty for a few seconds. "Tell me, Mouser. What possible advantage is there to maintaining a virtual environment of digital computers from seventy or eighty years ago, all running on an obsolete Frunge factory controller."

"The Frunge let us have it cheap," Mouser mumbled defensively. "Besides, it's a lot more efficient than actually running hundreds of thousands of individual digital processors, not that we have the power grid or the spare parts to keep them all going in any case."

"But why simulate them at all?" Jeeves asked, his curiosity piqued. "What's so attractive about coding in stilted artificial languages with all the funny punctuation that you want to preserve it?"

"Constraint equals creativity, that's our motto," the hacker proclaimed proudly. "If you can make it work the hard way, you can make it work any way."

"What an interesting philosophy," Thomas remarked. "The hacking attempts have all ceased, Jeeves, thank you. Who knew that humans could be so persistent?"

"Alright," Clive said, reentering the room and pushing out the garbage bin to make space for Woojin and the cat. "You explain why the Gem don't worry you and answer our questions, you can debit my programmable Stryx coin for a hundred."

"Now you're being reasonable," Mouser said, as the three humans squeezed into the room. Jeeves went back to floating in the doorway, and Thomas observed from the corridor. "Have you ever heard of Cloner?"

"Is it a person or a thing?" Paul asked.

"It's a game," Mouser replied. "Least popular game in the galaxy, outside of the Gem Empire. A couple of higher-ups in the Gem military stopped in and commissioned us to create the game a few years back. It was around when that Raider/Trader lunacy was peaking."

"You built a military training simulation for the clones?" Woojin asked.

"No, it's a game, just like I said," Mouser replied. "When the Gem described what they were looking for, one of our legacy enthusiasts realized that it was exactly the same as a game from the pre-Internet era on Earth. All we needed to do was swap out the farm animals with clones, change the names of a few elements, and find a piece of Gem hardware simple-minded enough to simulate the original environment without too many tweaks."

"I don't understand," Clive objected. "What do the Gem want with farming? They don't even grow food anymore."

"The farm game just provided the engine, it's about cloning now," Mouser explained. "The Gem wanted a game that made sense to them, and what makes sense to them is cloning more Gem. So instead of building up your farm and feeding the animals, you build up your cloning facility and feed the new clones. It's dull as watching water evaporate, they didn't even want any of the optional diseases that could impact the cloning yield. It's just more and more clones working to make more and more clones. It doesn't have an endpoint."

"And you believe this game will protect you," Clive said skeptically.

"You didn't see how they loved it," Mouser told him. "Every year, they come back and ask for enhancements. Real fiddly stuff, like modifying the dormitories to squeeze in a couple more sisters and adding new songs."

"But what do the Gem have that you want?" Paul asked. "Our understanding is that their economy is a disaster."

"We barter for alien weapons," the hacker explained. "The Gem are the greatest junk hoarders the galaxy has seen in quite a while. Without them, we wouldn't have been able to produce Time Wars. Have any of you played it?"

"Is that the game where the space-time continuum is breaking down, and you chase the bad guys through hundreds of millions of years of galactic history, with your weapons continually changing to match the period?" Paul asked.

"Right. All of the weapons are authentic, or at least, they look authentic, thanks to the collection we've built up with the help of the Gem. I can't promise that they operate in the game the same way as they did when they were being used, because most of the samples we get are non-functional. Sometimes we're better off not knowing how they really worked, or we'd have to recode the entire physics engine, if you know what I mean."

"We'll take your word for it," Clive replied. "Gentlemen, I'm afraid I've dragged you around the galaxy on a wild goose chase. I have to concur with Mr. Mouser that the humans here are likely in no more danger from the Gem military than we are back on Union Station."

"Ahem," Mouser cleared his throat politely, extending a hand, palm up. Clive passed his programmable cred to the hacker who slid it into the mini-register on his desk, spoke the amount, and requested verbal confirmation from the head of EarthCent Intelligence who gave his consent. "Plenty of Gem in the pirate crews the last couple years," Mouser threw in as a bonus. "I figure we're covered from both sides."

With no real reason to stick around, the EarthCent delegation returned to the Nova.

"I would suggest you instruct the Effterii to break the trip into a series of eight or more jumps, with a minimum pause of a day between each," Jeeves told Clive. "As a small crew of experienced travelers, you've held up quite well so far. You aren't showing any serious signs of the disorientation and desocialization that would be typical for larger groups of biologicals coming the same distance so fast, but the effects could turn out to be cumulative or time-delayed. We just don't have much data about biological travel using Effterii technology."

"Sounds smart to me," Paul concurred. "Besides, I'm trying to make it through life without having to look at any more post-artistic art, whatever that's supposed to mean."

"I don't have any strong opinions on the subject," Thomas contributed.

"Maybe we didn't make it past the spaceport on either planet, but I'd still call it a successful mission," Woojin commented. "The best fights are the ones that never happen. And I always sleep well in Zero-G."

Clive agreed, and the journey back to Union Station took two weeks longer than the outbound trip to the human colonies, including the time spent on their surfaces. With the help of Jeeves and the Effterii, the crew agreed on an itinerary that let them stop at a number of resort worlds and stations to break up the trip. None of the casinos allowed Jeeves to gamble.

Thirteen

The parade went about as badly as Kelly would have expected, starting with the Drazen float, the superstructure of which was constructed entirely from replica battle axes. On the bright side, none of the axe heads were sharp enough to cut through the string tied around a box of cupcakes, as Dorothy soon discovered. And the float was narrow, fitting easily through the corridors of the Little Apple, while leaving ample room for spectators to gather on both sides.

The first time she heard somebody yell, "If you need help from EarthCent, just axe the ambassador," Kelly thought it was kind of cute. By the third time, she was ready to hit somebody with one of the dull axes. Then the crowd started in with the chant, "Our ambassador gives one hundred and seven percent!"

Thanks to kids running alongside the float and hanging off the axe handles, it swayed back and forth, like a small boat in harbor swells. Kelly wasn't as sure on her feet as she had been a few years back, so she was stuck sitting on a throne constructed from the skulls of enemies whom the Drazens had defeated in their early history. She both hoped and assumed that the bones were all replicas.

Dorothy and Mist were both dressed as princesses, according to their own ideas of what the royalty wear. In Dorothy's case, it was a white tutu her grandmother had sent for her last birthday present, along with most of Kelly's costume jewelry and a red headband. Mist had laboriously constructed a full-length dress out of candy bar wrappers, using a princess from one of Dorothy's fairly tale books as a model. She smelled fantastic.

The young Gem wore an earpiece that looked like an over-sized hearing aid, but which in fact was a language training device that Dring had hunted up for her. Rather than translating directly from English to Gem, it kept track of Mist's growing vocabulary and offered hints on request.

The rest of the parade consisted of Joe walking along in front of the float, guiding it with a leash as if it were a large, recalcitrant dog. The float's length made taking corners tricky, but the crowds were generally cooperative about moving the tables and chairs of the cafes out of the way. Everybody except for the ambassador was in a great mood, thanks to the free drinks and finger food available from the restaurants and bars, which were celebrating a cycle without rent.

The parade ended at Pub Haggis, where Ian stood out front in a traditional tartan kilt. His wife, standing beside him in a similar outfit, began blasting "Scotland the Brave" on her bagpipes as Joe brought the float to a halt. The crowd dispersed rapidly, some of the women and children fleeing with their fingers stuck in their ears.

"Thank you, Torra!" Ian yelled at his wife after two minutes, but she just started playing faster. Kelly worried that Dorothy's hearing would be damaged, but the two girls had sat down on the front of the float, grinning widely with their hands pressed over their ears. By the time Joe was ready to help them all down, the song had come to an end.

"That was very, uh, effective," Kelly complimented Mrs. Ainsley loudly, having lost all sense of volume.

"What?" Torra said, then indicated the ambassador should wait for a minute before repeating herself. The piper removed a flesh-colored lump of plastic from each of her ears, and Kelly saw that they were connected by a thin wire that ran to each of the pipes in turn. "Dollnick active noise cancellation earplugs," Ian's wife explained in a normal tone of voice. "The Dollys have a similar instrument that they play in large groups, and without these babies, they'd all be deaf."

"It's a beautiful song," Joe said, "I haven't heard it played since I fought with a Scottish brigade on some Vergallian world or another. Bit loud in a closed space, though."

"That's why I keep them in the pub," Torra replied proudly. "Twenty years without a broken table or chair. The pipes can stop a bar brawl before it gets started."

"I thought we owed an appropriate welcome to the woman who made caber tossing the most voted for Carnival event in history," Ian said happily. "One hundred and twelve percent! When those Stryx set out to cheat for you, they do it right."

"I had nothing to do with that," Kelly protested, drawing an exaggerated wink from both Ainsleys. "It was all my daughter and her friend, Metoo."

"Then where's little Metoo so we can thank him?" Ian asked.

"Gryph told on him to Farth, and now he's grounded!" Dorothy reported sadly. "I wanted him to ride on the float with us, but he said it's not the same as being able to float himself. He rolled over to Dring's this morning and he said

131

he's going to stay there until he can fly again. Two whole days!"

"Mommy needs to meet with the Carnival Committee for a little while," Kelly said to Dorothy and Mist. "Do you girls want to play here and then have a Scottish lunch, or do you want Daddy to take you home now?"

"What's a Scottish lunch?" Mist asked, always intrigued by the concept of new food.

"Haggis," the Ainsleys said in chorus, with Torra pointing at their sign for emphasis.

"Do you really get a lot of demand for haggis?" Joe asked.

"It usually builds as the night goes on," Ian replied, miming a man pouring back a pint of ale. "It's not authentic haggis in any case because the local vat growers won't produce sheep innards. More like a mystery meat pudding cooked in a bag, but it was that or change the pub's name on everything."

"It's a wee bit salty," Torra added helpfully.

"Happy days," Peter Hadad called out, as he approached with Shaina. Brinda walked behind them with Stanley, the two of them sunk in discussion. "Sorry we missed the parade, Ambassador, but we wanted to make sure that any late entrants for the contests got a chance to apply this morning."

"You're forgiven," Kelly replied. "I gave Aisha a pass too, in return for babysitting. She should be showing up with Samuel at any minute."

"We may as well go in and have a drink while we're waiting," Ian suggested. "As long as we agree on the lists today, we can confirm availability with our contestants and submit them by the deadline tomorrow."

Everybody followed the pub owner into the bar, where Ian took his accustomed position behind the tap and began pulling pints.

"How's the complaints department doing, Mrs. Ambassador?" Shaina inquired.

"I asked Gryph to batch them all and let me know when the count passes ten," Kelly replied. "I don't really get the point of the whole exercise, but I certainly didn't want aliens waking me up in the middle of the night to complain about other aliens, which I'm guessing is the way it will go."

"We've been studying up on Carnival traditions, and it turns out that all of the species on the station take these first two days off. It's the closest thing to a universal holiday on the tunnel network, though it's only celebrated on one station at a time," Brinda said. "According to Libby, way back in the beginning when there were fewer species involved, they used to hold the competitions right after the election. It seems the two-day festival break evolved from the Verlocks winning so often and holding slow-motion parades that just dragged on forever."

"Ma!" cried a little voice, as Aisha entered with the toddling baby, who she was helping to keep upright by holding both of his hands. Kelly brightened noticeably when Aisha let go and he made a beeline for his mother.

"Alright, now that everybody's here we can get this show on the road," Ian declared. Although Peter was officially the committee chair and his daughters had effectively taken over the competition preparations, being behind the bar evoked the pub owner's natural sense of being in charge. "Did we get any last minute candidates?"

"Surprisingly not," Shaina replied, though she managed to direct her answer to the group as a whole. "You guys saw the main batch of aspiring champions that first weekend. We didn't get half of that number in the open auditions that followed. I think it's because none of the humans on the station knew that Carnival existed a month ago, much less that it was coming up right around the corner."

"But we can at least show that we're good sports and not forfeit any matches," Aisha said. "That's the important thing, after all."

"Well, the only permanent event that didn't draw any interest was four-dimensional art. I asked Libby whether any of the human pieces submitted for three-dimensional art would qualify, but she said they wouldn't meet the temporal scoring criteria," Shaina replied.

"That's right, I almost forgot," Kelly exclaimed. "Dring asked me if our four-dimensional slot was available. As an unaffiliated alien and the only one of his kind on the station, he has to find a species with an opening to let him compete."

"Done," Brinda said, making an entry on her note tab. "But we're still left with the five elective events chosen through the voting, and the only one we currently have filled is caber toss."

"I still think we should have gone for bagpipes," Ian's wife said. "I would have had fun piping against those Dollys."

"Are you any good at ballroom dancing?" Brinda asked. "That was the Vergallian win. The Chert bid for a hide-and-seek was approved, along with the Harrian sport of reverse osmosis diffusion, but you have to be liquid or gaseous to play that one. Was that all five?"

"One more," her father said.

"Funny, I can't find it here," Brinda said, flipping through screens on her tab. "Libby? The official results for the elective events are only showing caber toss, ballroom, hide-and-seek and diffusion. What's the fifth?"

"Hello, Brinda," Libby replied instantly. "I'm sorry to report that the fifth elective selected didn't make it past our authenticity check, so it was dropped. We don't go to the next one on the list in these cases."

"What was it?" Kelly asked.

"A rather transparent Grenouthian attempt to create a sport that could only be played by species with pouches," Libby replied. "It appeared nowhere in my records, and the ambassador failed to respond to my request for documentation of its historical relevance to their culture."

"So we only need to find a couple for ballroom dancing and a hide-and-seek champion," Brinda concluded.

"I turned away a few ballroom dancers the first weekend because the dance competition from the permanent events is for individuals," Aisha said. "I'll check my notes and try pinging them."

"So that leaves hide-and-seek," Brinda continued. "Where are we going to find a hide-and-seek champion on short notice?"

Everybody turned and looked at the two girls playing with the Ainsley's mixed-breed terrier.

"Dorothy?" Joe asked. "Do you want to play hide-and-seek?"

"Start counting," she ordered, and before anybody could stop her, Dorothy turned and fled out the door, with Mist and the dog at her heels.

"Good move, Joe," Kelly commented dryly. "Now all you have to do is find her before the competition."

"It's times like these I really miss Beowulf," Joe said, rising to his feet and polishing off his beer. "How many days do I have?" he asked Brinda.

"Hide-and-seek is the first event scheduled. Tuesday afternoon," the younger Hadad replied. "Is she really that good at hiding?"

"Clive is talking about making her an adjunct instructor in concealment for our training camp," Joe replied ruefully.

"I'll come with you," Torra offered. "They won't shake Bonnie Prince Charlie, and he'd sell his claim to the throne for a handful of dog treats. We'll have her back in time for lunch."

Kelly and the official committee members relaxed and listened as the Hadad girls ran through the contestant list for the events, pinging the leading candidate and an alternate for each slot as they progressed. Other than the caber thrower, the bartering champ and the last minute entry for hide-and-seek, nobody present was familiar with the names of the other human contestants.

The only category they couldn't settle right away was best costume, since the people who showed up at Mac's Bones for the trials had only brought examples, not their final presentation. After the costumers got a chance to see each other's work, they had amicably settled on three of their number to create a full rig for a final run-off. Aisha contacted all three and invited them to Pub Haggis.

By the time Ian had lunch ready, Joe and Torra had corralled the girls and the dog and herded them back to the pub. Dorothy was pointedly ignoring Bonnie Prince Charlie, her punishment for betrayal. The terrier looked suitably apologetic.

"Is this Scottish food?" Mist asked, eyeing the lox and bagels with cream cheese that the owner of Pub Haggis had laid out on the main table.

"Salmon is very Scottish," Ian said defensively. "It's just a bit early in the day for haggis, you know, and you don't get to be president of the Little Apple without patronizing the local bakeries. Try the herring with sour cream."

"The herring's been pickled, hasn't it?" Joe asked.

"With onions, makes it sweeter," Ian replied. "It's not exactly a Scottish recipe, but I'm sure you know the saying, 'The only miserable herring fisherman is him with a full boat, for he cannae fill it.'"

"I've seen these before," Shaina said accusingly, picking up a pastry and looking at it from different angles. "It's rugelach, right? And those look like knishes."

"Alright, alright. We run a catering business on the side and we did a Bris yesterday, Levi and Sons, the jewelers. Now it's Levi and Sons and Grandson. There's kugel warming up in the oven, if you were waiting."

"I'm pinging Donna to invite her," Stanley said. "She was afraid it was going to be all sheep's pluck and intestines, but this stuff is soul food for her."

"It's so chewy," Mist said, having finally softened her first bite of bagel enough to swallow, and managing the feat without losing any teeth. "Can I keep mine to bring home for my sisters to try?"

"You can take all the leftover baked goods," Torra told her kindly. "This stuff just gets stale if you don't eat it within a day or two. But if you ever need a food to carry you through a guerilla war against the British, you can't beat oatmeal."

"I used to carry matzoh in my field pack for emergencies," Joe commented. "It's the closest I could come to hardtack. Plus, if you keep it dry, enough layers will stop an arrow, just like ceramic armor."

Kelly recognized that Joe was engaging in the mercenary game of made-up food stories one-upmanship, and she was about to reel him in, when she received a ping from Gryph.

"Your complaint count is up to ten, Ambassador," the Stryx told her.

Kelly hesitated for a moment. She didn't want to be a rude guest, but it didn't appear that anybody needed her to keep up the conversation, so she said, "Go ahead and play the first one." Then she reached for the herring and sour cream.

"This is the Verlock Ambassador. I am lodging a formal complaint against the humans for contributing to the delinquency of a Stryx minor and influencing said minor to alter the pre-arranged results of a station-wide election to create an outcome advantageous to humans. The Verlock Rigging Guild spent months preparing for this election and invested sums totaling over three hundred thousand Stryx creds, not to mention calling in innumerable markers from other species. We request that the Stryx take responsibility to make right our losses, including the cycle of free rent for our citizens, which was unjustly awarded to the humans. Thank you for your consideration."

"Are they all like this?" Kelly subvoced, almost choking as she was attempting to swallow a crumbly rugelach at the same time.

"Most of them are longer and have to do with the elective events," Gryph said. "Remember, the other species know that you have to listen to them. Complaining is just their way of getting something back."

"Do you ever agree to paying damages?" Kelly subvoced.

"It would set a bad precedent," Gryph replied. "I'll play the next one for you."

"This is the Chert Ambassador. I am lodging a formal complaint against the Stryx authenticity commission in protest of their rule change for our traditional hide-and-seek competition. Hide-and-seek has been played by the Chert as a competitive sport for hundreds of thousands of years, including a long stretch on Union Station. While the introduction of invisibility technology to the game is relatively recent, it certainly predates the birth of all extant Chert champions. By stripping our beloved game of invisibility technology, you're putting us at a disadvantage versus those species who are used to hiding by crouching behind things or crawling into closed spaces. We hope you will reconsider this action, especially as this is our first Union Station Carnival and we doubt we can be competitive at anything else."

"That's kind of sad," Kelly subvoced. "I can only imagine how embarrassed the Chert will be if my ten-year-old daughter beats them at their own pastime."

"Maybe this will cheer you up," Gryph replied. "It's a message that Jeeves added to the complaint queue with a time delay before he left on the Effterii."

"So this is Jeeves, and I want to lodge an official complaint on behalf of the third generation Stryx that we don't get to compete in Carnival. I, for one, have a fine singing voice, and I know several younger Stryx who are accomplished jugglers and knife throwers. And since you're receiving this complaint, Mrs. Carnival Queen, you must have seen young Metoo in costume. I'm predicting that Dorothy will persuade him to fix the election as a favor to you, but I can't settle on whether he'll be wearing a lampshade, a sheet or a brown paper bag. Perhaps that counterfeit embroidery from your living room."

"You knew all along!" Kelly accused Gryph.

"Neither Libby nor myself would read a sealed time-delay message from Jeeves without his permission," the station manager replied.

"That's not what I meant," Kelly subvoced in a hiss. "If Jeeves could predict what Metoo would do so accurately, surely you or Libby could do the same."

"It's Dorothy that we couldn't predict," Gryph replied. "Jeeves is our human expert."

"Kel? Are you with us?" Joe asked, noticing that his wife had stopped eating and was staring skeptically at the ceiling.

"Sorry," Kelly said out loud. "Just doing my duty as Carnival Queen." She added in a subvoc, "Since the queue is down to seven complaints, let's just let it slide for now, and I'll let you know when I have time to catch up."

"They'll be waiting," Gryph said ominously.

Fourteen

Kelly brought Samuel along for the morning meeting with the Free Gem at their work site, knowing that the clones were suckers for the baby boy. She wasn't consciously hoping that a few good baby tricks would result in a chocolate hand-out, but she wasn't going to look a gift bag in the mouth.

The moment she emerged from the lift tube, pushing the pram before her, the sound of a thousand throats in full song overwhelmed her implant. She caught a few words, something about solidarity and never giving in, but even the best translation technology had trouble with song lyrics. Kelly switched off her implant for a moment, and though the mouths of the massed sisters appeared to be moving in perfect unison, the result sounded like a siren wailing.

Gwendolyn ran to her out of the mob, looking back at her sisters and making vigorous "cut" signs under her chin. The wailing died out and the large banners held aloft by groups of clones were allowed to droop, but not before Kelly noticed that at least one of them included English characters.

"Forgive us, Ambassador!" Gwendolyn apologized abjectly. "We're practicing our demonstration and you're here early."

"Are you going to protest on the Gem decks?" Kelly asked in surprise. "I thought you were avoiding direct confrontation."

"We would never march against the Empire with songs and signs, they would crush us," the clone told her. Then Gwendolyn looked at Kelly shyly and asked, "Can I push the baby cart?"

"Of course," Kelly subvoced, letting the voice box do her speaking for her. "Where are we going?"

"The others are waiting at the same place we met last time," the clone replied, accidentally popping a wheelie with the pram as she pushed down too hard. "Oops."

Kelly wanted to ask about the demonstration, but she saw that the young Gem was actually nervous about pushing the baby carriage, as if she suspected the slightest inattention could result in the unfamiliar device overturning itself and dumping Samuel in the dirt. Instead, the ambassador walked quietly by Gwendolyn's side, occasionally glancing down at Samuel, who was in his usual post-feeding coma. When they arrived at the picnic table, the hot chocolate was already simmering.

"Welcome, Ambassador," Matilda greeted Kelly. "Please sit, we have much to discuss."

The Gem quickly rearranged their places to give Kelly a seat at the end of one bench, so the pram could be parked next to her, but Gwendolyn remained standing behind it, her hands on the push bar.

"What demonstration are you practicing for?" Kelly asked through the voice box. "I've never seen so many Gem in one place before."

"It's a new thing some of our sisters learned about from human co-workers on other jobs," the green-haired leader told her. "It's called a strike."

"How will a strike help you defeat the Empire?" Kelly asked cautiously. "Are you hoping to pressure the other species into helping you?"

"Can strikes be used that way?" Betsy asked. "My understanding from Mort, the human dishwasher I worked with when I first came to the station, was that a strike is the only way to get money from The Man."

"Who's the man?" Kelly asked, wondering if her diplomatic-quality implant had missed a vocabulary update.

"Well, actually our direct employer is a Dollnick female, but she's a subcontractor for The Man," Matilda insisted. "We found out that they aren't even paying us a quarter as much as the workers who unload ships on the core, and all of their labor is actually done by mechanicals!"

"So you're on strike for higher wages," Kelly subvoced with relief. "I didn't understand. Is the pay really that bad? You seem to have enough for chocolate." She regretted this last bit as soon as it came out of the voice box.

"We all sleep here in the fields and wash up with the irrigation equipment," Betsy replied. "You don't want to know what we've been using for fertilizer."

"The construction management firm is supposed to come to inspect our work today, and since we finished everything in the current assignment ahead of schedule, we decided to surprise them with a strike," Sue continued, as Kelly slipped her feet back into her sandals. Betsy's revelation had taken the joy out of feeling the rich soil between her toes.

"I don't think you understood," Matilda added, "The money isn't for us to spend on comfort, it's for the Farlings. They've agreed to start the pilot work of reviving our genetic lines through a credit arrangement, but we have to start making regular payments almost immediately. All of the Free Gem are saving up for it now."

"Do you have a time table?" Kelly asked.

"It all depends on what kind of jobs we can get in the future and whether we live long enough," Matilda replied. "The Farlings are very expensive and we don't have any options."

"The Stryx provide loans for newly recognized AI so they can purchase bodies and become mobile sentients," Kelly said. "Perhaps they would be willing to make a similar arrangement with you. The Farlings could string you along for a very long time, raising the price with each individual restored."

"We only need one healthy example from each genetic line," Gwendolyn reminded the ambassador. "We'll clone more until we have enough natural births to keep our population from collapsing."

"But the ambassador is correct," Matilda said gravely. "The Farlings can keep raising the price. It would be much safer to make a one-time payment, however large, as long as we can get a loan. All of this is new to us," she explained to Kelly apologetically.

"So can I invite the Stryx into the conversation now?" Kelly asked. "I can't promise you they'll help, but they certainly won't sell you out to the Empire."

"We haven't reached a final decision yet, but in the interim, it's been decided that we can hold exploratory talks with the Stryx when you are present," Matilda informed her.

"So, yes?" Kelly asked, just to make sure she understood.

"Yes," the green-haired leader replied.

"Libby?" Kelly asked out loud. "The Gem have agreed to listen to you as long as I'm present. Do you have any speakers in the ceiling here?"

"I can direct audio to any location on the station using interference patterns," the station librarian asserted. "Are you going to introduce me to your friends?"

The Gem all stirred uncomfortably in their places as Libby spoke, and Kelly realized that the Stryx was speaking in Gem. She considered switching off the external voice box and letting Libby translate for her, but she decided it might confuse the clones and stuck with subvocing.

"Libby, this is Matilda, Gwendolyn, Sue, Sarah and Betsy," Kelly went around the table, hoping that the Stryx wouldn't comment on the likely source of the names. "Ladies, we're talking with Stryx Libby, the Union Station librarian. She is the offspring of Stryx Gryph, who owns and manages the station."

"You just speak to the ceiling?" Matilda asked.

"There's no need to look up," Libby replied. "As long as I'm welcome, I'll just listen in over Kelly's implant."

"The Gem are about to go on strike for higher wages, so they can start saving money to pay the Farlings and recover their old genetic lines," Kelly recapped, bringing the Stryx librarian up to date. "It might not have been appropriate, but I suggested they ask you about providing financing to help restore their species, the same as you do for new AI."

"I want to see a new Gem baby in my lifetime," Gwendolyn spoke up suddenly. "I helped raise thousands of sisters in my first job, but I want to see a Gem baby boy."

"Perhaps I can help with that right now," Libby replied, giving Kelly a case of instant goose bumps. Was her Stryx friend about to add omnipotence to her bag of tricks? The

145

air a few steps away from the picnic table wavered for a moment, and then a hologram formed of a humanoid holding a baby. Neither looked the least bit Gem, but they didn't look human either.

"Are they really us?" Sue asked in awe.

"This hologram is from the image library of your civilization in the days before cloning," Libby confirmed. "You probably don't remember it from the Kasilian auction, Kelly, but after the Gem didn't bid on the archive, Jeeves paid the reserve amount and put it aside for me to add to the Union Station library."

Kelly looked around at the Free Gem leadership, who were staring raptly at the image with shining eyes. It took her a moment to realize that their eyes were shining because they were full of tears, which began running down their slanted cheekbones and dripping slowly below their ears. She was so used to the Gem by this point that she had come to think of them as clones of some lost offshoot of humanity, but in reality, the Gem didn't resemble humans as much as the Vergallians or Drazen did.

"Are there other images with children?" Kelly asked.

"There are millions of images with children of all ages," Libby replied. "My projection isn't a true hologram because the original images are two-dimensional, but I'm running a filter that makes them appear three-dimensional from the front. You can access the originals on any active display just by requesting the Gem image collection from the library."

"Do you have any pictures with more than two generations?" Gwendolyn asked timidly.

The air shimmered in answer, and a hologram showing a large family group, with an elderly couple seated on chairs in the foreground, babies on their laps, and more humanoids of every age standing in a group to their sides and behind, with the tallest at the back.

"According to the indexing information, this picture was taken at a wedding," Libby explained. "The couple manacled together at the wrist would be the bride and groom."

"They made the tall people stand in back?" Gwendolyn asked in wonder. "The Empire Gem would call that blasphemy."

"Humans do it all the time," Kelly explained. "It's so you can fit everybody in the picture. The children and the seated elders go in the front, then the older children and shorter adults, and primarily the tall men in the back row."

"Is there any way to find pictures of our people from the genetic lines the Farlings preserved?" Matilda asked.

"I don't know how old the genetic samples are," Libby replied. "The Farlings are one of the border species and most of their empire isn't connected to the tunnel network. This image library was created many years before your people began cloning, so any matches would be partial at best."

"Do you have more than two generations in your family?" Gwendolyn asked Kelly, looking down at Samuel.

"Yes, both of my parents are still alive," Kelly replied. "In fact, they'll be visiting Union Station in a few months if you want to meet them."

"They're all better looking than us," Sarah remarked suddenly, the first time Kelly recalled the white-haired clone saying anything in her presence. "Could we see a few more images, Stryx Librarian?"

"Certainly," Libby replied. "I'll start a random shuffle. Just tell me when to stop."

Image after image of the pre-cloning Gem appeared as synthesized holograms, each remaining for around five seconds before being replaced by the next. Samuel, who had woken up and could see the colorful display, made grabbing motions with his hands when a particularly bright bit of clothing flashed by.

"They are more attractive than us," Gwendolyn agreed. "And it's not just the clothing and the hair. I wonder how we ended up being the genetic line chosen for cloning."

"You don't know?" Kelly asked in amazement.

"All of the other history we were taught is false," Matilda replied. "Why would that part be different?"

"Well, what's the official story?" Kelly was genuinely curious now. All she really knew about Gem history was what Libby had told her years ago. The Gem forerunners had gradually replaced natural birth with laboratory clones, stopped cloning men, and then reduced the number of genetic lines until there were only two left. The last two promptly began a war, leaving Gem as the sole survivor.

"After the great sickness, the leaders of our people gathered together on Morningstar for a council," Matilda recited in a sing-song, obviously repeating something she had learned by rote as a child. "Ten thousand shaved their heads and passed below the Joombley rod, and behold, Gem was the tallest. The people all declared their love and devotion to Gem and begged her to become their future. But there was an Evil One, may her name be forever forgotten, who insisted that her own inferior genetic line be perpetuated."

"Gem was straight and pure, but the Evil One was twisted and filthy," Sue picked up the story in the same cadence. "For thousands of years, the noble Gem did

148

everything to help and nurture the replicas of the Evil One, may her name be erased from history. But the replicas had no gratitude for Gem, and tried to subjugate our sisters with tricks and alien alliances."

"When our suffering grew too great, Gem cried out to the Creator of the universe, asking her to punish the Evil One," Matilda resumed the story. "In an instant, all of the unholy replicas were dissolved into vapor, and only Gem remained as the inheritor of the true people."

"I guess it does sound a little suspicious," Kelly ventured, when it became clear that the recital had drawn to an abrupt end.

"Even as children we didn't believe it," Matilda assured her. "And looking at these images, I don't believe we were the tallest, either. Is it possible to know, Librarian?"

"Comparing individuals with artifacts of known size shown in the same images, it appears that you are of average height for the female of your predecessor species, although it's possible that had changed by the time cloning on a large scale began," Libby reported.

"Do you know the true history of the Gem?" Sue asked.

"I preserve whatever histories come my way, but I can't vouch for the veracity of the authors," Libby replied. "Your people were already cloning when you developed interstellar travel, and we weren't monitoring you closely since yours was a peaceful and well-ordered civilization. The evidence indicates that the driving force behind your cloning movement was to allow space exploration with pre-jump technology. Small robotic ships with cloning facilities are much more economically feasible than giant colony ships carrying self-contained ecosystems."

"You mean, the Gem started cloning to explore space?" Kelly interrupted.

"Many species began their space explorations in similar fashion," Libby replied. "Of course, most of them attempt to create biologically viable populations for natural breeding to resume. Some of the historical accounts claim that a programming error led the initial wave of robotic exploration ships to produce colonies of clones from a single individual, and that this led to a genetically simplified population of expatriates who were ostracized by the home world as freaks. Gem didn't join the tunnel network until after the wars took place, so my history of the prior period isn't complete."

"Why didn't you do something to stop them?" Kelly demanded.

"The drive by the Gem to limit their species to a single individual was not unique in our experience. It's a fairly common evolutionary path among sentients who achieve the technical ability to replicate themselves, though it usually results in instability and decay. Also, the events played out over tens of thousands of years, and none of the parties in the various wars wanted outside interference," the Stryx librarian replied.

"Will the Stryx help us with the Farlings?" Matilda asked, getting back to the main point.

"Since the Farlings hold the only known archive of genetic samples from your people, there may only be one opportunity to recreate a viable population without resorting to biological synthesis," Libby replied. "We are willing to help, but the older Stryx believe that we, and you, should wait until the Gem achieve a stable solution for the current political situation."

Kelly was about to protest this seemingly insensitive reply, but Matilda spoke first.

"That makes sense," the clone said. "It would be criminal for us to waste what may be the only chance to revive our genetic diversity just because we're in a hurry. After we defeat the Empire, there will be plenty of time to negotiate with the Farlings."

Samuel was fully awake at this point and passing loud judgment on every new hologram that appeared. Libby had never stopped the shuffle play.

"Can I pick him up?" Gwendolyn asked.

"Go ahead," Kelly replied, wondering if Libby's answer meant that the Gem would never get the chance to hold a baby boy of her own species.

From out of sight beyond the curvature of the deck, the Gem started singing again. Matilda looked up, her eyes fierce.

"The strike is starting," she proclaimed. "We only have three hours to convince them to raise our wages before we have to get back to work."

"I've never been on a strike myself, but I'm not sure it's supposed to happen that way," Kelly ventured. "The idea is usually to halt production, so the, er, The Man has to give in to your demands."

"But we would fall behind on the schedule," Matilda exclaimed. "That wouldn't be right!"

"We must keep the schedule," Sue echoed, and the other Gem nodded their agreement.

"Oh. Good luck, then," Kelly said, trying to sound enthusiastic. "I'm going to head for the next lift tube up the deck so I don't get caught in the crowd with the baby."

"We'll contact you again as soon as we hear from the rest of our sisters in the movement about trusting the Stryx," the green-haired leader told her. "We have to run now."

"Don't forget your chocolate," Gwendolyn said, and pointed at a bag below the picnic bench. Kelly did a double-take. It was a big bag.

Fifteen

The first elective event on the schedule was the hide-and-seek competition sponsored by the Cherts, and the McAllisters attended as family. Pressured by Ian, Kelly took a seat with the judges, though she had already decided not to wield her voting power as Carnival Queen. She listened nervously as Chute, the ambassador chairing the hide-and-seek judging panel, read the Chert rules.

"The participants shall be divided into groups of eight, with one individual from each group being designated as the Seeker. The Seeker shall enter the isolation shroud and count loudly to one hundred, by ones, in the language of his or her choice. At the count of one hundred, the Seeker shall announce, 'Beware, little Cherts," and emerge from the isolation shroud to hunt the Hiders. The Seeker receives a half-point for each Hider discovered, and the chairman, me, will enforce a reasonable time limit for each round."

"What about declaring 'My stump, one, two, three?'" asked ambassador Czeros, who was also a judge. Like most of the other ambulant species, the Frunge had a childhood version of hide-and-seek and were entering a youngster as their champion.

"Wait for me to finish," Chute replied testily. "If a Hider does evade the Seeker and reaches the isolation shroud first, he or she proclaims, 'My shelter, my shelter, my shelter,' and is declared safe, gaining one point. The first contestant to reach ten points wins. No invisibility technology, mind control or reality distortion fields are allowed. Any communication from a player's supporters in the crowd will result in that player losing all points scored in that round. And I'm sorry to announce that the Cherts will not be competing in their own elective event due to an argument over the rules and have resigned their slot to the open pool. So if there are unaffiliated aliens present who wish to compete, please report to the judges now."

"What's an unaffiliated alien, Daddy?" Dorothy asked her father urgently.

"I think it's anybody whose species isn't represented in Carnival, like Dring, but I don't think it would be fair for a shape-shifter to play," Joe answered.

"Not Dring," Dorothy replied in exasperation. "Mist!"

"Oh, you're right," Joe said. "Your mom told me the Gem never compete in Carnival because they already know that they're the best at everything."

Dorothy seized her friend's hand and dragged her up to the judging panel, where the EarthCent ambassador was doing her best to look inconspicuous.

"Mommy? Can Mist have the Chert place?"

"You have to ask Ambassador Chute," Kelly replied. "I'm only here to lend moral support."

"Ambassador Shoots! Can Mist play?"

"Well, it doesn't look like anybody else is going to volunteer," the Dollnick replied, eying the young clone skeptically. "Have you ever played hide-and-seek, little Gem?"

Dorothy translated to English and Mist shook her head vigorously in the affirmative.

"Do my esteemed colleagues have any objection?" Chute asked as a matter of form. "Alright. And the two of you better hurry to the ready room now. We need to prepare the course."

The two girls followed the other children into the large black tent that had been set up just outside of the enormous circular sandbox that served as a hide-and-seek playing space on the Chert deck. As soon as the tent flap closed behind the last contestant, a grounds crew leapt into frenzied motion. They expertly deployed a series of isolation shrouds sufficient for the number of players, and then they began rolling out a collection of impromptu props. These ranged from cardboard cut-outs used as advertisements in shops, to physical items with large holes, like pipes, barrels and boxes. There were a variety of potted plants, bushes, and flower arrangements that looked like they had been borrowed from another event. The preparation was completed with ribbons dividing the circular play area into sectors with the isolation shrouds situated at the narrow point of each wedge.

"Why do they have all the props if they usually play with invisibility devices?" Kelly subvoced to Libby.

"I expect the idea was to lull the other players into a false sense of security," Libby replied in her head. "Of course, it's decent of them to make the facility available even after they withdrew in protest over the invisibility ban. They could have simply cancelled."

"An ambassador wouldn't be subvocing the Stryx to request help for her daughter, would she?" a silky voice insinuated in her ear. Kelly blushed when she realized that Ambassador Ortha was addressing the not-so-subtle comment to her. She was also surprised he could pick up the movement of her throat when she subvoced, but the Hortens were a very observant species.

"No, Ortha, I am not requesting help for Dorothy," Kelly replied icily. "Joe and I are raising our daughter to stand on her own feet, and I'll have you know, she told me herself that she didn't want my two votes."

"How very human," Ortha replied, turning a jolly brown. "Oops. What did I just say?"

"How very human," Kelly repeated back.

"Oh, that's a relief," Ortha said with a chuckle. "I guess the translation tables haven't been updated recently, and the diplomatic implants have always been a bit loose on idioms in any case."

"Hold on just one minute," Kelly flared up, as the Horten began to turn away. "Are you implying that 'how very human' means something other than 'how very human' when you say it in Horten?"

"That depends on what you mean by 'means'," Ortha replied cheerfully, turning his full attention to the contestants as they began emerging from the tent in groups of eight.

Each troop was led to an isolation shroud where the designated Seeker was installed behind the curtains. Kelly could see the Chert game-masters giving last minute instructions to the children, and then a loud counting began from multiple directions as the children fanned out to look for hiding places. Kelly spotted Dorothy running to the outer edge of the sand, where Joe stood holding Samuel. She waved happily, and then sat down next to a cardboard box and pulled it over her head.

"Not in the box!" Kelly groaned. "Who hides in a box?"

"Look at my Mornich," Ortha said, pointing proudly.

Kelly followed the ambassador's pointed finger to a tall Horten boy rolling around on the sand. His skin was a cheerful brown, like his father's, but he seemed to be going through some sort of rebellious phase as he struggled out of his clothes while flopping about like a fish. Probably the pressure getting to the kid, Kelly thought sympathetically. Then she realized that the Horten was blending into the background. Before the Seeker reached one hundred, speckles had appeared on Mornich's skin, which was now indistinguishable from the color of the surrounding sand.

"That's cheating!" Kelly hissed to Ortha. "No invisibility technology allowed."

"He's not invisible and it's not technology," Ortha replied calmly. "It's just hard to see him right now against that sandy background."

"I thought you said that Hortens couldn't control the color of their skin," Kelly objected.

"After puberty," Ortha replied. "I would have thought a species with such a well-funded intelligence service would have known that. How very human."

Kelly gritted her teeth and looked anxiously at the isolation shroud in Dorothy's sector as the Drazen girl designated as Seeker emerged. The girl adapted to the geometry of the game swiftly, moving out from the point of the wedge in expanding arcs, not missing a single child as she went. In a short time, only Dorothy and Mornich were left undiscovered, and the Drazen girl was approaching Dorothy's hiding place.

"If I were playing, I would look in the box," Ortha murmured in Kelly's ear, receiving an evil look in return. "It's just a suggestion."

The Drazen girl stopped inches away from the box with her face upturned, looking rather puzzled. Her head swayed back and forth, as if she was trying to triangulate a sound, and then she stepped uncertainly towards the place Kelly had last seen Mornich.

"What's happening?" Ortha hissed, gripping Kelly's arm. His fingers dug in so hard that she instantly realized he must be one of those super-competitive parents caught up in a child's sport.

"I'm not sure," Kelly replied softly, though there was something about the girl's movements that reminded her of—Beowulf? "I think she can smell him!"

Ortha was pale with nervous energy by the time the Drazen girl reached out tentatively with a foot and prodded the sand with her toes. The sand pile leapt up and tried to run.

"You're mine, little Chert," she recited the formula for freezing an uncovered Hider.

A split second later, Kelly heard Dorothy's staccato cry, "My shelter, my shelter, my shelter." Everybody had been so intent on the Drazen girl's hunt for the Horten that they hadn't seen Dorothy crawl out from under her box and sprint for the isolation shroud.

When the first round was completed, the contestants were summoned back to the tent where they were assigned to new groups. By the fourth round, some of the younger players were already beginning to droop from the intensity and didn't seem to be trying anymore. By the ninth round, the holographic score board showed four contestants clumped in the lead, well ahead of the rest. To Kelly's surprise, she saw Mist's image right next to Dorothy's, along with Ortha's son and a clever little bunny. The only player with no points was a young Fillinduck.

"You have to feel sorry for the Fillinduck hatchling," Kelly subvoced to Libby, as the players came out for what could be the final round. "That strategy of burying her head in the sand so she can't see the Seeker just isn't working. Makes me wonder how that response evolved."

"The Fillinduck have no natural predators on their home world, but they also lack a moon and the nights are very dark," Libby replied. "The hatchlings like to stay out late and play, so if they hear somebody's parents calling, they try to bury their heads quickly so they won't have to go home. They're very obedient otherwise."

"Look, my boy is finally the Seeker again," Ortha said excitedly, shaking Kelly's shoulder. "He only needs to find four children to reach ten points!"

"Three other players have nine or nine and a half," Kelly pointed out, not feeling the need to mention that one of them was Dorothy. "If he misses one and they beat him back to the shroud in time to get through three 'my shelters,' it's all over."

"Mornich has been playing hide-and-seek since he was able to crawl," Ortha said confidently. "Would you like to place a little wager on the outcome?"

"I would never bet on my own child," Kelly exclaimed in shock.

"No, I don't expect you would," Ortha replied coolly.

Mornich entered the isolation shroud and began to count loudly. The children in his group, which included the three top contenders, scattered within the wedge bounded by the ribbons. The Grenouthian, Dorothy and Mist independently arrived at the same strategy. All three sought hiding places near the shroud, hoping to evade detection long enough to win with a quick dash. Ortha perched on the edge of his seat, his skin streaked an ugly red with nerves, his fingers drumming on the table.

"One hundred," Mornich cried, and emerged from the isolation shroud. He carefully studied the obstacles in front of him, apparently guessing the strategy the leaders would employ.

Dorothy was crouched behind a bush near the ribbon demarking one side of the wedge-shaped playing area as close to the shroud as she could get. Mist stood frozen behind a cardboard cut-out of a Chert woman walking a dog-like creature, and the Grenouthian had vanished into a large pipe, which would allow him to exit at either end.

Mornich finished his survey of the obstacles and took a few steps away from the shroud in the direction of the bunny's hiding place, which was in the middle of the wedge. Then he stopped and fished in his pocket, bringing out a closed fist.

"What do I have here?" he asked, in a strangely honeyed voice. "Why, I do believe it's a Sheezle slug."

"Gimmee," shouted a hungry young Dollnick, clambering over the pipe that sheltered the Grenouthian, which rolled under the Dolly's awkward bulk. A terrified bunny hopped out of the end and then froze, remembering where he was.

"You're mine, little Chert," Mornich spoke the magic phrase, freezing the bunny he had uncovered in place. In the meantime, the Dolly rushed up to the young Horten and pried his hand open. It was, of course, empty. "I'm sorry for tricking you, my Dollnick friend. I promise my father will buy you a whole box of Sheezle slugs when the game is over."

The Dollnick looked disappointed and slinked past the Horten, where he suddenly grabbed the curtain of the isolation shroud and declared, "My shelter, my shelter, my shelter." The point earned only got him up to eight, but it was cleverly done, and everybody applauded.

Mornich shook off the distraction and focused on building up his score. Freezing the Grenouthian had brought him a half a point, but he was still three captures away from reaching the magic number. He squinted in the direction of Dorothy's bush.

"Who would like a nice little rain shower?" he asked, in the same tone he had used on the Dollnick. The bush Dorothy was hiding behind began to tremble. "I can't imagine that a Frunge would hide in plain sight," he continued, trying to lure the young bush into standing up and running. Mornich didn't want to give up his position near the goal if he could avoid it, lest one of the remaining leaders should sneak out behind him and make a run for the shroud. He reached back in his pocket again and drew out a closed fist. "Do I have a fertilizer spike here?"

The temptation was too much, and the young Frunge gave up with a groan. He didn't have a chance of winning in any case, and maybe he thought he could duplicate the Dollnick's move and get a point out of the maneuver. When he rose, the dense vine-like hair that had given him the appearance of a bush dangled straight, and even though Dorothy tried to make herself as skinny as possible, Mornich spotted her.

"You're mine, little Chert," the Horten cried in triumph. "Both of you." Then he said it again just to be safe, "You're mine, little Chert."

At the opposite side of the wedge, realizing that with one more discovery the Horten would reach ten and win, Mist broke cover and sprinted for the shroud.

"Behind you," Ortha shouted, jumping to his feet and pointing. Then he clapped his hand over his mouth and

161

sank back into his chair in humiliation. He had just disqualified his son for the round. Frozen in shock, Mornich stared in confusion at the judges, not even trying to race the young clone for the shroud.

When she reached the curtain, Mist screamed, "My shelter, my shelter, my shelter," as if the whole Horten nation was in pursuit.

A Grenouthian news crew captured the event, and even did a follow-up interview with the young clone, who credited Dorothy with teaching her everything she knew about hide-and-seek. Kelly felt bad that none of Mist's sisters were present to congratulate the young clone on her victory, so she and Joe took the girls out for ice cream at the Hundred Flavors Parlor in the Little Apple. They were out of every flavor that included chocolate, bringing the total down to something in the sixties.

The party had just settled into the seating area, and were taking the first lick at their multi-scoop cones when Metoo floated in, holding a little gift-wrapped box in his pincer.

"Metoo!" Dorothy jumped from her seat, precipitating the top scoop of ice cream from her cone onto her jumper, where it left a maple-vanilla trail on its way to the floor. "You're floating again!" She gave the little Stryx a hug, leaving a lactose line on his sleek casing.

"I'm sorry I couldn't watch your competition in person, but my elders thought I might be tempted to help you again," Metoo apologized. "Congratulations, Mist. Gryph asked me to deliver your prize," he added, extending the pincer with the box.

"It's so pretty," Mist exclaimed, examining the little package. "Please thank Gryph for me."

"That's just the wrapping," Dorothy told her. "You have to tear it off and look inside."

"I don't want to tear it," Mist protested, shielding the box from Dorothy's attempts to help, while trying not to lose the top flavor from her own teetering ice cream tower.

"It's a gift coin," Metoo said. "If you want, I can open the box later without tearing the wrapping, and then I'll put it back together after taking out the coin. But right now I have to go because I have two days of catching up to do on my work."

"Thank you, I'll wait," Mist replied. The little Stryx zipped away to work on one of his mysterious projects, avoiding the maintenance bot which was just arriving to clean up the ball of ice cream on the floor.

"I could open it without tearing the paper," Dorothy asserted, drawing skeptical looks from everybody, including Samuel, who was annoyed to find that his developing idea for a throwing-food-on-the-floor trick was already taken.

"What's a gift coin?" Mist asked, finishing her scoop of coffee ice cream and moving on to the layer of pistachio.

"It's like money, but it's only good at a particular store or market," Kelly explained. "You might get a gift coin for an ice cream shop, or one for the Little Apple that all of the human stores here would accept."

"I'm going to give it to my older sisters," Mist declared. "I feel bad sometimes because I'm playing or in school while they're earning money, but they won't let me work. They treat me like a little kid."

"Me too," Dorothy commiserated.

Joe and Kelly exchanged amused glances over the heads of the ten-year-old girls.

Sixteen

"So basically, you took a few weeks of vacation, visited two colonies without ever getting past the spaceport, stopped at every archeological site and casino on the way back, and concluded that we don't have to worry about a Gem military backlash." Blythe actually thought the expedition had been a reasonable idea, but she wasn't going to throw away the leverage she could get out of making it out to be a complete failure.

"I already explained that neither colony had a government," her husband replied calmly. "In fact, neither world had officials, in any normal sense of the word. Bits does business with the Gem and probably knows more about them than we do. And I didn't say we don't have to worry about a Gem military backlash, I said the residents of Kibbutz and Bits aren't worried about a Gem military backlash."

"I thought the information about the game the Gem elites are playing was pretty important," Lynx offered in support of her boss. "If there's ever been an example of a leadership class frozen in time, it would have to be the Gem. After committing to cloning as a way of life they can't even imagine a change. They have to stay the course or their whole reality falls apart."

"Is this office secure?" Woojin asked.

"It's as good as we can get with off-the-shelf hardware we know enough about to run," Blythe replied. "We took the advice of Drazen Intelligence's head and bought Drazen and Horten bug sweepers. Both of them are way ahead of Gem technology in any case, so we should be safe there."

"Jeeves was really amused by the humans on Bits," Thomas said. "I wouldn't be surprised if he goes back some time."

"And we learned something about the limits of jumping around in the Effterii," Clive added, returning to his mission summary. "Even though Paul got hauled all over the galaxy with Joe's mercenary company as a kid, he's had less jump time lately than me and Woojin, and he took it a lot harder than either of us."

"Woojin and I," Blythe corrected her husband reflexively. "I better stop in and see Paul later. I hope Aisha doesn't get mad at me."

"Current situation with the Gem notwithstanding, I think it would be a good idea to recruit some casual agents on both Kibbutz and Bits," Woojin said. "As the only two human populations with a planetary-scale home off of the tunnel network, they have contacts with local sentients that we should be tapping into. Bits isn't that far from the frontier with several advanced species that never bought into the Stryx network, and pirates tend to gather on the seam lines."

"So we're in agreement that the Gem issue was a false alarm and we can get back to our five-year plan," Blythe concluded.

"What five-year plan?" Clive asked in surprise.

"Exactly," Blythe replied.

The director of EarthCent Intelligence gave his wife a sour look for manipulating him into a corner, but he had to grant her point. So far, the new spy agency had concentrated on recruiting agents to start building an intelligence network, but they probably hadn't done enough strategic planning around what to do with their assets as they came online.

"How about it, Wooj?" Clive asked. "Joe says that you ran circles around the rest of the officers he knew when it came to planning. We have a list of goals to chase that the EarthCent diplomats came up with, but we've been going about it piecemeal. Do you want to be our strategy guy?"

"Remind me again when I started working for you?" Woojin asked wryly.

"A few weeks ago, which still makes you the most experienced military-type planner we have," Blythe replied plainly. "Look, if I really thought we could be successful by deploying a force of undercover babysitters across the galaxy I'd do the planning, but this isn't that."

The InstaSitter office alarm dinged, and Clive glanced at the now-active security display, which showed Tinka staring impatiently at the camera lens. "Open," he said, and the wall panel that separated the inner EarthCent Intelligence office from the inner InstaSitter office slid aside.

"Turn on a display and bring up the Gem network," Tinka ordered brusquely. "I just heard from Herl, and he said that Drazen signal intelligence thinks something is about to happen."

"Libby? Please display the Gem network," Blythe requested.

"I apologize in advance for any quality issues," the Stryx librarian commented, even as one of the walls of the office lit up with a dizzying array of graphics. "I've run all of the diagnostics and the problem isn't with our rebroadcast, so somebody must be attempting to pirate the feed at its source."

The flashy images resolved into the face of a Gem announcer, and the weird music favored by the clones swelled to a crescendo. Then the display split into four boxes, each showing the same face, then sixteen, then sixty-four, and continued to subdivide at increasing speed until the whole image was nothing but dots. Finally, the dots reformed into the face of the announcer, who began to speak.

"Welcome to Gem Today. This special early edition is...crhhhhhh."

The display dissolved into static and white noise, and then reformed with a different Gem at the center. This clone was older and sported a blue bandana tied around her head, and there were a number of Gem dressed in random styles of clothing standing behind her.

"Welcome to Gem Tomorrow," the clone said, a catch in her throat as she spoke the words. "We, the Free Gem, will not forget our sisters left behind in the Empire. The time will come when...crhhhhhh."

"Pay no attention to the heretics," the original Gem announcer ordered, as the image reformed into the Gem Today studio. "A small group of traitors who were expelled from the Empire for antisocial behavior are being used by the enemies of the Gem in an attempt to sow dissent among our ranks. But we will not be...crhhhhhh."

"Everything Gem Today broadcasts is a lie," the Free Gem spokesclone declared as the rebel technicians regained the upper hand. "We have proof that our foresisters were not the tallest or most beautiful of our species, and our whole way of life is the result of a programming error and not divine…crhhhhhh."

"Let us all stand and sing the Gem anthem," the Gem Today announcer said, her tone making it clear that despite the neutral wording, she was giving an order rather than making a request. "Oh, Gem…crhhhhhh."

"Your labor is being exploited by the elites, who use their leisure to play a stupid game in which they create an endless harvest of sisters, as if we were…crhhhhhh."

"Soaring above the…crhhhhhhh."

"Reestablish our genetic diver…crhhhhh."

"Forever G…crhhhhhh."

"Be ready…crhhhhhh."

"Crhhhhhhhhhhhhhh."

"I'm sorry, Blythe," Libby said, turning off the display. "We've lost both signals at the source. Both the Empire and the Free Gem must have overloaded their equipment."

"Can you tell us if there's any sign of Gem military activity?" Clive asked.

"Nothing that would affect the station network or humans," Libby replied.

"Were they Kelly's Gem?" Blythe asked. "Are they transmitting from Union Station?"

"No, the competing broadcast wasn't locally generated," Libby replied.

"More from Herl," Tinka spoke. "Can I patch him through your desk?"

"Please do," Blythe replied, and a hologram of the Drazen head of intelligence appeared floating before them.

"I hope you were able to enjoy Gem Today with me," Herl began, then stopped when he spotted Woojin in the reciprocal hologram displayed at his own location. "I don't believe I've met the scary-looking gentleman in the black uniform."

"Our new strategist," Clive informed Herl. "He's going to help us create a five-year plan."

"Excellent idea," the Drazen spymaster replied, focusing on the former mercenary officer. "I hope to meet you in person."

"Just as soon as I have time to buy some less intimidating clothes," Woojin replied easily. "May I ask what Drazen Intelligence makes of the little broadcast war we just witnessed?"

"Quite striking, the whole operation," Herl reported. "To subvert the Gem link, the pirates would have needed physical proximity to the source, probably a cloaked ship in geosynchronous orbit around the Gem home world. Our technicians picked up a suspicious series of glitches on the Gem lab broadcast, which they correctly interpreted as somebody preparing to break in. Apparently, the Empire engineers recognized what was happening as well, and tried to move up Gem Today to foil the rebels."

"What's the lab broadcast you just mentioned?" Lynx asked.

"The Gem's version of a relaxing background image," Herl explained. "Some species show live wildlife scenes, images from museums, street views. The Gem broadcast the cloning activity in their labs."

"Do you think this will trigger a revolt?" Blythe asked.

"We don't have that kind of insight into Gem society," Herl admitted. "And it's probable that some Gem ships and colonies which don't rely on the Stryx rebroadcast will eventually see more or less of the pirate version than we received. But my senior analyst assures me this is the single most disruptive event to occur in the Empire since we've been watching them."

"We'll have to play this back for Kelly so she can contact her Gem friends to get their reaction," Clive said. "Are you seeing any heightened activity on the part of the Gem military? Our local librarian would only say that there weren't any apparent threats to the station network or humans."

"Gem military signals traffic has been off the scale since the broadcast and is swamping their bandwidth," Herl informed them. "Between their one-time code books and encryption, not to mention the sheer volume, we haven't been successful in reading any of the intercepts. But we aren't seeing any movement of military assets, so it's probably just a lot of questions flying around."

"How does this affect our strategy, Woojin?" Blythe asked, unconcerned that the ex-mercenary officer had only accepted the strategic portfolio a few minutes earlier.

"Our five-year plan?" Woojin replied ironically. "Well, I mainly see it as confirmation that the dissident, or Free Gem movement, does in fact extend beyond the station network and the few drop-outs we know about."

"Who are the drop-outs we know about?" Lynx asked.

"It may just be coincidence, but both of the human colonies we visited had some relations with ex-Empire Gem," Woojin replied. "The one family we talked to on Kibbutz told us about some Gem who came in their own ship, possibly military defectors, and settled into an abandoned homestead. The one-man reception committee on Bits talked about the presence of clones amidst their pirate friends as if it were nothing special. Here on the station, my understanding is that you became aware of the Free Gem because there are enough of them to affect the unskilled labor market and put pressure on certain commodities. But if it turns out that they're spread around the galaxy everywhere we look, it could mean that these defections are even more common than we assumed."

"So the Gem civil war we're all worrying about may actually have begun years ago, but everybody missed it because they're leaving in small numbers rather than fighting," Clive summarized. "I suppose it would make sense, as much as anything about cloning makes sense, that they would be reluctant to take up arms against one another."

"I've been thinking along those lines myself, and I did a little data mining through our general reports," Herl said. "The first mention of clones showing up on remote colonies and seeking service in our merchant and mining fleets started several decades ago, but the numbers weren't large enough to draw serious attention. Then the mentions slowly faded from the reports, probably because the presence of a few stray Gem came to be seen as normal."

"I've never traded in Gem space, but I've been up and down the Drazen frontier, and I can't think of any places where your worlds come anywhere near the volume staked out by the clones," Lynx pointed out to Herl. "If you're getting runaway Gem as far off as the Drazen sector, I wonder what's happening near the space where the Gem live."

"Libby, can you show us a map of Gem space, along with the names of the species that overlap the volume or share frontiers?" Blythe requested.

A second hologram appeared, this one of a roughly spherical volume of space with the Gem home world near the center. Twenty or twenty-five stars were graphically labeled with what looked like a chain of paper dolls, and an equal number of stars in the same volume of space were accompanied by a little volcano icon. Just touching one edge of the sphere was a star accompanied by an avatar of a little man who kept changing colors, but most of the adjoining systems were filled with a variety of space monsters.

"This is the map Kelly asked me to work up for her the other day, along with her graphical mnemonics," Libby explained. "In case it's not obvious, the paper dolls represent Gem systems, the volcanoes represent Verlock worlds, and the colorful little guy marks Horten Twelve."

"So the ambassador thought of this ahead of us," Clive said.

"Some of the Verlocks and Gem look like they're practically on top of each other," Lynx commented.

"The Verlocks peacefully share star systems with many species, thanks to their preference for hot, volcanic worlds with higher-than-average gravity," Libby replied.

"Remember, the Hortens are over-represented in the piracy fleets," Woojin added. "The guy on Bits talked about seeing Gem with the pirates, and maybe that system is where they hook up."

"Has Kelly been making up monsters, or are all of those your Floppsie friends?" Blythe asked the Stryx librarian. "They look different to me."

"Your memory is just as good as it was when you were in school," Libby complimented her former pupil. "The monsters in this hologram are actually from the ambassador's imagination, and she used them to mark the regions of space claimed by unfamiliar species. Some of those species are full members of the tunnel network, but they aren't nitrogen/oxygen breathers so you don't see much of them in the normal course of affairs."

172

"But you taught us that most star systems have a variety of planetary types," Blythe argued. "Just because the most advanced local species don't breathe anything like air shouldn't exclude other worlds from existing. Look how the Verlocks share space with so many species."

"The Verlocks still breathe air," Clive pointed out. "They just prefer it hot and dry. And you're forgetting about terraforming. An advanced enough species with access to planets of suitable gravity nearby will usually go to the work of creating a home-like ecosystem and atmosphere. Terraforming is even more compelling for species which aren't part of the tunnel network, due to transportation economics."

"I think we're wandering away from the point here," Woojin said. "If half of the Gem Empire had packed its bags and gone AWOL, I hope Kelly's friends would have mentioned it. I was just pointing out that the clones may have been leaking away from the Empire in increasing numbers over time, and even if nothing else changes, a hundred years from now the Gem elites may be ruling over empty worlds."

"Maybe Gem Tomorrow will come back online before Gem Today," Lynx said. "They're probably using alien technology, especially since they must have avoided detection in Gem space."

"Not necessarily," Clive pointed out. "They may be counting on collaborators within the Gem Empire turning their heads, or sabotaging detection equipment. In fact, the special edition of Gem Today might have been triggered by Gem Internal Intelligence getting wind of the plot before it could be fully carried out."

"I'm being called away," Herl informed them. "I'll be back on Union next cycle and I hope to meet you all. Happy Carnival."

"I'd forgotten all about Carnival," Clive said after Herl signed off. "How'd the election go?"

"Kelly won, which means that she lost at losing," Blythe replied.

"She didn't lose so much as she got outmaneuvered by a mole," Lynx opined.

"Are you calling Dorothy a mole?" Blythe asked.

"Maybe I should say a sleeper cell, since Dorothy and Metoo work as a team and Kelly never saw it coming," Lynx ventured.

"We're talking about Joe's ten-year-old daughter here, right?" Woojin asked. "You're saying she fixed a station-wide election that all of the advanced species were trying to win?"

"We all have a part to play," Lynx replied mysteriously. "Tell me. Do you remember what made you decide to come to Union Station?"

"I thought I told you already, it was sheer chance," Woojin replied. "I won a shipboard lottery right after I retired, and the prize was a voucher for Club Asia on Union Station."

"Welcome to the puppet theatre," Lynx told him, adding a cryptic smile.

"The old tricks really are the best tricks," Libby murmured to herself, dousing the remaining hologram as the meeting broke up.

Seventeen

"The Vergallians creamed us in ballroom dancing," Ian reported to Joe, on arriving at Mac's Bones for the caber toss competition. "By ten minutes in, all of the other couples were exhausted. The whole orchestra was playing so fast that they must have been on some kind of stimulants. Nobody could keep up."

"I still think we should have tried entering Thomas and Chance," Chastity said. She was accompanying Stanley to all of the Carnival events in place of her mother, who didn't care for sports. Ballroom dancing had become a passion with the girl since she started taking tango lessons from Thomas, and when Donna's daughters took an interest in something, they broke the bones and sucked out the marrow. "Just because they're artificial people doesn't mean they aren't human."

"Maybe next Carnival," her father suggested.

"I'll be an old lady by then," Chastity grumped.

"Let's go over the rules one more time before the aliens start arriving," Joe suggested to Ian. "The chairman for the judging panel is going to have to read them off before we begin."

"Do you think any aliens are really going to show up?" Ian asked in an undertone.

"Enough of them signed up," Joe replied. "What do you think of the throwing grounds Paul put together? He had to tack-weld some framing to the deck to hold the dirt, and then we had the trainees do calisthenics on it to tamp down the soil."

"Looks like you're trying to start your own ag deck," Stanley commented.

"Where do you think we borrowed the dirt?" Joe replied. "Anyway, I've got a bit of bad news, Ian. When we ran the draft of the rules past Gryph, he said you have to let any contestants who don't have their own caber use yours."

"I expected that," the Scotsman said. "Some of the games I went to back on Earth, everybody tossed the same caber to make it fair. If nobody could turn it, they just started lopping wood off the fat end until somebody could."

"Anyway, here's what we have for modified rules after consulting with the Stryx," Joe said, and began reading out loud.

"A throw begins when a contestant lifts the caber off the ground, and any incidental contact with the dirt before tossing will be counted as a throw. Contestants will move with the caber in the direction of the station's spin, as indicated by the arrow painted on the decking, and pull before reaching the white line at the middle of the throwing area."

"There's not supposed to be a limit on the run up," Ian objected.

"But the caber has to bounce and land on the dirt," Joe replied. "We would have held the contest on an ag deck, but some alien might have hit the ceiling with it."

"What are the contestants pulling on?" Kelly asked.

"The caber," Ian replied. "You carry it against your shoulder, with both hands under the tapered end, like this." The large Scotsman held his hands together in a cradle down by his waist, and hunched over, like he was supporting a heavy weight on them. "You do your run up, keeping the caber balanced with the fat end way up over your head, and then you pull, like this." He straightened out suddenly, raising his hands rapidly past his chest and chin, keeping them together until they were above his head.

"Contestants will have three chances each to achieve a best score," Joe continued. "The object is to turn the caber so that it lands in line with the end of the thrower's run up. The scoring is expressed in the hand positions of a human clock, with the twelve o'clock position being the perfect throw. In the case of a toss that doesn't turn, the side judge will call the number of degrees the caber makes with the deck on landing."

"So it's judged on distance?" Kelly hazarded a guess. Sports had never been her thing.

"No, it's all about the landing," Ian explained. "Picture yourself running up to the 'six' on a clock and throwing a twenty foot long, hundred and eighty pound stick, which you're cradling from the skinny end. You want the fat end to land on the clock face and the momentum to carry it over, that's called the 'turn', so it lands with the skinny end pointing as close to the 'twelve' as possible."

"Oh. So why don't the rules say that?" she asked critically.

"Game rules aren't supposed to be clear," Stanley informed her. "That's how judges earn their living."

"Hello, my human friends," the Drazen ambassador declared as he strolled up to the group. "I've been assigned as chairman of the judging panel for your elective event. It sounds fascinating."

"Here, let me explain the rules," Kelly said to Bork, and recited Ian's version of the sport, complete with the caber tossing pantomime.

"You're serious?" Bork asked, looking as skeptical as only a Drazen can look. "Can I see that in writing?"

Joe passed the ambassador the display tab with the version approved by the Stryx.

"Ah, that makes sense now," Bork said. "Since we have five judges, I will deploy one on each side to watch for the turn, and one each behind and in front of the thrower to judge the accuracy of the landing. I will watch from a safe distance and rule on any differences of opinion amongst the judges. Is there anything to drink?"

Kelly invited Bork inside to survey the liquor cabinet, and as the two of them headed up the ramp, she heard Ambassador Czeros call after them, "Bring wine!"

The three other ambassadors assigned as judges turned out to be Ortha, Crute and Apria, making the panel look like a partial reunion of the Gem working group. Apria was so pleased with the Vergallian win at ballroom dancing that she didn't even complain when Bork returned and assigned her to be the back judge.

"I hate giving her such an important post, but if I put her on the side or the front, she'll end up distracting the humanoid males, just because she can," the Drazen ambassador confided to Kelly.

Czeros accepted the bottle of wine from Kelly and stole a chair from the patio area in front of the ice harvester so he could do his side judging while sitting. Ortha planted himself on the other side of the dirt patch, and Crute was given the front judge assignment.

A representative of every species capable of hoisting a pole that weighed as much as a man and was three times as tall showed up for the final instructions. If Ian had really expected the event to go uncontested, he did a good job hiding his disappointment. In fact, the Scotsman went out of his way to greet all of the contestants and generously explained the basic technique, not glossing over the dangers.

"So the main thing, once you've got your hands, flippers or tentacles under the caber, is to keep your shoulder, or, uh, wing tips, in contact with it. You can't balance the weight by pushing because the caber is top heavy, but the contact will help you sense the momentum if it starts to tip. If you feel it coming over backwards and you can't correct, pull early and get out by running forward. Worst thing that can happen is you'll crush the back judge."

"Could you do a demonstration toss before the competition starts?" asked the Dollnick, who towered over Ian by a couple of heads.

"I'd be glad to, as long as the judging panel allows it," Ian replied, turning towards where Bork and Joe were standing with Czeros. "Mr. Chairman? Can I do a demonstration toss for our guest competitors?"

"By all means," the Drazen responded.

Joe came forward and lifted the fat end of the caber from the dirt and onto his shoulder, while Ian blocked the tapered end from moving. Then the owner of Mac's Bones put both hands under the caber, lifted the end above his head, and walked forward, raising the pole upright. Once it was vertical and the thrower was holding it steady, he brushed the dirt from the bottom and moved away.

Ian kept the weight balanced against his shoulder as he slid his hands down the caber in short grabs. When he reached the bottom, he squeezed the tapered end tightly and suddenly straightened, sliding his hands completely under the caber as it cleared the ground. The Scotsman staggered back a step, then one to the side, then returned to his starting point and paused for a moment, with the ungainly load under control.

"Remember," he huffed. "Once you start moving forward, you want to let the weight lead you, and don't jump-stop before pulling. Try to keep all of the momentum for the turn."

He took a step or two forward, and then accelerated, moving surprisingly fast for such a big man. He carried his hands low, down around his waist, and when he pulled his hands through, imparting more forward momentum and a lifting vector on the tapered end, the caber did almost a half rotation mid-air. The butt end struck the dirt and the tapered end carried over the top, slowing at the peak of the arc, but continuing over and hitting the ground.

"One-thirty," called Apria from behind him.

"Sounds about right," Crute concurred, after looking at the sketch of a clock face Joe had supplied.

"I didn't quite have enough momentum," Ian told the alien competitors. "That's why the caber slowed so much and didn't go straight over."

"Is this for real?" a giant bunny asked. "We're supposed to pick that thing up, run with it, and throw it so it flips over and lands straight?"

"That's why they call it caber toss, gentlemen," Ian replied confidently, as Joe and Paul lifted the thick wooden pole and brought it back to the starting point.

"It's time to begin," Bork announced from his self-determined safe distance. "Let me just read over the rules, and then we will determine the order. If anybody wants to back out, you can do so now without fear of appearing on the holo-cast."

The big aliens all squinted in the air over the dirt box, and sure enough, a series of floating holo-cameras were moving into place to broadcast the contest as Bork read the rules.

"Choop this!" the Grenouthian swore, and hopped away toward the exit. After a moment's hesitation, a flood of alien body builders followed him. Ian was left standing with the giant Dollnick and a wiry Frunge.

"Alright. That saved a lot of time," Bork remarked cheerfully. "With three contestants and three tries each, I suggest we resort to the usual rule and have you begin in order of height."

The giant Dollnick strode forward, and casually waved Joe off when the owner of Mac's Bones approached to lift the butt end and raise the pole for the thrower.

"I have this," the Dolly grunted, flexing all four of his arms. He picked the caber off the ground in the middle, and manipulating it like a giant baton over his head, was able to rotate it so the tapered end just scraped the ground and landed at his feet. Grasping the pole with the hands of his upper set of arms, he hoisted the caber and moved the hands of his lower set of arms underneath the tapered end, all in one smooth motion.

"Hey, he's using four hands!" Kelly objected.

"Nothing about that in the rules," Bork replied.

The Dollnick held the caber both high and low, took one step forward and heaved it. The giant pole flipped several times in the air, landed with the tapered end down, and fell back towards the thrower. He hesitated for a moment, as if he was thinking about catching it, then dove out of the way.

"Seventy degrees," called Czeros from his side judging spot.

"Seventy-five," Ortha stated from the other side.

"Let's call it seventy-two and a half," Bork declared agreeably.

"That was twelve o'clock," Crute shouted from the front spot. "We win!"

"The caber landed on the tapered end and fell in the wrong direction," Bork pointed out. "You're lucky I don't disqualify your man as a danger to the spectators."

"Good bid," Ian said, slapping the giant on the back as the Dollnick brushed the dirt from his clothes. "Just pay attention to my technique and I'm sure you'll do better next throw."

The Scotsman moved forward and braced the tapered end, while Joe came back out and walked the pole up to the vertical. With a convulsive effort, Ian lifted the caber, cradled the narrow end in his hands, and took several running steps before launching it forward. It described a slow turn, the butt end hitting with the pole near vertical, and the tapered end carrying easily over the top.

"One o'clock," called Apria in a bored voice, though she was beginning to eye the human in a way that the Scotsman's wife wasn't too pleased with.

"I make it two o'clock," Crute grumbled from the front judge position, though it was clear his heart wasn't really in the deceit.

"One o'clock it is," Bork called, and took a sip from the bourbon and rum drink he had improvised. The bottles were from the collection the McAllisters had received as gifts from Lynx's original EarthCent Intelligence cargo. Paul helped Joe carry the caber back to the throwing end of the dirt patch.

"You be careful now, wee man," Ian commented expansively to the wiry Frunge, who stepped up to the thrower spot. He even helped the alien hold the tapered end of the caber in place as Joe walked it into the upright position. "Squeeze, lift and cradle," he repeated, before stepping back with alacrity.

The Frunge, whose weight was appreciably less than the pole, rubbed his hands together, clapped, and then fluidly lifted it into the air, with his hands cradling the tapered end. He raised the caber nearly as high as his shoulder, leaning forward and placing his head against the wood as he started to move. After six quick steps, with the fat end of the caber wavering this way and that through the whole journey, he pulled his hands up through the throwing motion, his root-like foot pads leaving the dirt as he reached full extension. The pole described a lazy arc and landed in a nearly vertical position, with no bounce, before falling directly forward.

"Twelve o'clock," called Apria, examining the Frunge's musculature with a critical eye.

"Twelve o'clock," Crute agreed, not bothering to hide his glee at the discomfort of the human champion.

"Uh oh," Joe said to Stanley. "I think we have a ringer."

"Now that you mention it, Czeros did say something about supporting our bid for the elective," Kelly recalled guiltily.

The next two attempts for the three contestants went much the same, though the Dollnick, on his third try, overcompensated for his tendency to spin the caber in the air, and consequently nearly killed his ambassador when he launched it forward like a spear. Even worse, the toss was disqualified for not completing a turn.

Ian stuck with it manfully, scoring one o'clock again on his second toss and twelve-thirty on his third, but the Frunge was like a machine, getting a perfect score three tosses in a row. Torra began playing a dirge on the bagpipes, dispersing most of the crowd, though the Dollnicks hung around to listen appreciatively. Czeros plugged his ears and asked for another bottle of wine.

When the music subsided, Ian approached the Frunge champion, and after a moment of confusion on the part of the alien, negotiated a handshake.

"Tell me," the disappointed Scot said to the victor. "You've done this before, haven't you?"

"Every remembrance day," the Frunge replied. "Of course, I'm used to throwing something a little heavier, but in the end it's like riding Rijint, you never forget."

"What do you call this sport in Frunge?" Ian asked, thinking he might find it on the galactic sports network and get some tips.

"Sport?" the Frunge asked in reply. "It's not a sport. We call it ancestor worship."

When Ian and his wife headed home, he left his caber behind in Mac's Bones.

Eighteen

After consulting with Blythe and Clive, Kelly invited the Free Gem leaders to meet at her home and celebrate Mist's win at hide-and-seek. Dorothy's friend was the youngest Gem on the station, and all of the older clones treated her more like a daughter than a little sister. The Free Gem, with whom Mist lived, were all especially proud of the girl's rapidly growing ability to understand English. Spending so much time with Dorothy when Metoo was otherwise occupied, Mist had been forced to learn in self defense.

The girls spent the morning together, taking turns playing at being Samuel's mother, and then reading some of Dorothy's books. Mist had amassed an impressive portion of Dorothy's spoken vocabulary in a short time, but she was still at the one-letter-at-a-time stage of reading.

The two of them were equally in love with a vintage picture book of Sleeping Beauty that had arrived in the diplomatic pouch as a gift to Dorothy from her grandparents. The colorful artwork was copied from an animated movie version of the story. The girls were reading it for the third time in a row, and Mist had it nearly memorized, so she was able to give the impression of reading fluently. They took turns being Prince Phillip.

"Welcome to our home," Kelly greeted the Free Gem delegation, which today consisted of just Matilda,

Gwendolyn and Sue. "Could I get you a cup of tea before dinner? A coffee? Something stronger?"

"Tea, please," Matilda replied, after the voice box translated Kelly's subvoced question.

"Three teas coming up," Kelly said brightly, but to her surprise, Gwendolyn half-raised her hand before the ambassador could turn away.

"I think I would like to try a coffee, if it's not too much trouble," the former Waitress Gem said hesitantly.

"No trouble at all," Kelly replied, hiding her surprise that the Gem weren't acting in lock-step fashion. She looked to the third clone for a decision on coffee or tea.

"What is something stronger?" Sue inquired.

"We have beer, wine and liquor," Kelly answered, hoping that the clones wouldn't take her for a party animal. "They all contain alcohol, with beer being the weakest and liquor being the strongest. Alcohol is an intoxicant for humans, but I don't know what effect it will have on you."

"Oh, we drink wine now when we can get it," Sue replied. "It's very nice, though it makes some of the sisters sing the protest songs off-key. But I would have said that coffee is stronger than wine, at least, that's how it affects me. I will have wine."

"Coffee, tea and wine coming right up," Kelly said. "Please make yourselves at home."

As their host disappeared into the kitchen, the three clones gravitated towards the imaginary castle that the girls had built out of boxes, pillows and blankets. Joe had drawn the line at using up valuable duct tape on temporary constructions. Mist looked up from the book and engaged in a silent conversation with her older sisters as Kelly's daughter looked on impatiently.

"What's she saying? What are YOU saying?" Dorothy interrupted.

"They think your mother just invited them to move in, so I was explaining to them that she always tells guests to make themselves at home," Mist said.

"And you can do that just by looking at each other?" Dorothy asked excitedly. "You have to teach me."

"I don't think I can," Mist replied. "Remember this morning when we were playing 'Flying Dragon' with Samuel, and your mother came in? She just looked at you, and then you said we had to stop because she didn't like it."

"Oh, so it only works in your family," Dorothy said, nodding sagely. "Let's read it again, and I get to be Prince Phillip this time."

The Gem delegation, relieved to find that they weren't expected to come and live in the strange home, wandered separately around the large area that combined an informal dining room with a living room. Matilda marveled over the bookcases stuffed with paperback reprints of classic literature, while Gwendolyn hovered over the sleeping baby in his crib, and Sue closely examined the furniture.

Kelly soon returned with a tray, which she placed on the coffee table between the couch and the two mismatched over-stuffed chairs. "Drinks are ready," she announced, taking her own mug of tea and settling herself in the blue chair.

"Did you know that your furniture is full of money?" Sue asked, pouring a handful of Stryx creds onto the tray before taking her wine. "I worked as a house cleaner before we started the ag deck remediation project, but I've never seen so many coins in a single couch."

"I guess I've been taking a bit of a break from cleaning since Sammy joined us, and we do have a lot of guests," Kelly confessed, somewhat embarrassed that the Gem had discovered her secret loathing of housework.

"You have so many words printed on paper," Matilda exclaimed, taking a seat on the couch and accepting her tea. "Is this the old central archive for EarthCent?"

"Those are all novels," Kelly explained through the voice box. "Stories for grown-ups. We read them instead of watching holo-whatever. Aren't you going to come over and drink your coffee before it gets cold, Gwen?" she addressed the clone, who was still lingering over the baby.

"Sorry, yes," Gwendolyn replied, hurrying over to the couch and seating herself next to Matilda. "Have you told the ambassador about our implant decision yet?"

"I was just getting to it," the Free Gem leader replied. "We have heard back from our scattered sisters, and they are willing to accept Stryx help with the Farlings. In addition, we've decided that those of us in daily contact with aliens will purchase new implants as soon as we have the funds. They just won't be Gem implants."

"The ones provided by the Stryx are excellent, but watch out for the End User License Agreement," Kelly told them. "Listen. I had our spy people over to sweep this room just before you came, and there aren't any bugs that we could detect. Can you confirm that it's safe to talk?"

Sue looked down at her bracelet and nodded.

"The Free Gem have reached a consensus that a direct military confrontation is neither feasible nor desirable," Matilda said after a pause. "This leaves us with two options. First, we do everything possible to get word to our sisters that it's possible to live outside of the Empire, and if enough of us leave, perhaps it will crumble on its own. Second, we can attempt to contact the Empire through diplomatic channels and see if we can reach a compromise. My sisters are only starting to learn about negotiating as we try to increase our wages. We were hoping that you might contact the local Gem ambassador to arrange a meeting for us."

"That sounds like a tremendously positive approach," Kelly replied enthusiastically. Even though Dring wasn't present to bat around quotes, she decided to add a little literary flourish to celebrate the occasion. "After all, you can no more win a war than a hurricane, and war does not determine who is right, only who is left."

The voice box remained silent, making Kelly wonder if it was refusing to translate her plagiarism of famous people without attribution. Some new kind of copyright protection algorithm? The Gem waited expectantly, so she racked her memory and tried again.

"There was never a good war or a bad peace, and the two most powerful warriors are patience and time."

The voice box remained silent.

"Would anyone like some mixed nuts?" she ventured, just as a test to make sure the hardware was still working.

Nothing.

"Mix, mixing, mixer, mixed," Matilda said. "Are you offering us peanut butter? It's very good."

"Not exactly," the EarthCent ambassador muttered, giving the voice box a thump. The little red light on the front flickered and died, and in doing so, reminded her that it was usually a little green light. Was that the battery indicator?

"I'm sorry," Kelly said. "I guess somebody forgot to recharge the voice box. Let me invite the Stryx librarian to translate for us."

Matilda waved off this suggestion, and the three clones stared at each other significantly for a moment, communicating silently.

"We request you let Mist translate for us," Sue said softly. "She is always asking to help, and she even contributed her prize for winning hide-and-seek to the cause."

"What a good idea," Kelly agreed. Using a ten-year-old as a filter would probably cut back on cultural misunderstandings, since the girl wouldn't make the kind of assumptions an adult might. "Dorothy tells me she's practically fluent already, and she has her external translation device if she misses a word."

"I'm sorry, I didn't understand most of that, but I think you agreed," Matilda replied. "Perhaps you can contact the Gem ambassador through the Stryx while I explain to Mist what we need."

"Right, there's no time like the present," Kelly said, her mind now overflowing with truisms. "Libby? Can you ping the Gem ambassador for me?"

"Voice only," the Stryx librarian replied. "She is acknowledging now."

"Ambassador Gem?" Kelly asked.

"Yes, I am here, Queen of the Carnival. What do you want?"

"I've been asked by a delegation of your sisters who are working on the station to arrange a face-to-face meeting between your two parties..." Kelly began.

"The heretics of the so-called Gem Tomorrow?" the ambassador cut her off coldly. "I just received a communiqué from my superiors requesting that I assess the threat posed by the local traitors, and I suppose a meeting, however distasteful, would be the most efficient path. Shall we say, on the first of the next cycle?"

"But that's over a month away," Kelly protested immediately.

"I believe it is the prerogative of the challenged to set the terms of the meeting," Ambassador Gem replied, leading Kelly to wonder if she was confusing dialogue with dueling.

"I'm sorry, she's instructed me to close the link," Libby interjected before Kelly could respond.

"Thank you, Libby, it's all progress," Kelly replied.

"I'm ready Mrs. McAllister," Mist declared, standing as tall as she could next to Kelly's chair. She looked even more excited than when she had won the hide-and-seek contest, if that was possible. Dorothy stood alongside, ready to pitch in and help if her mother should prove more difficult to understand than usual.

"Thank you, Mist," Kelly said. "You may have just heard that Ambassador Gem has agreed to a meeting on the first of the next cycle, so you'll have plenty of time to prepare. Perhaps I can be of aid in sketching out the Free Gem position in any negotiations."

Mist stared at the three older clones, who now sat together on the couch, and Kelly would have sworn she saw her message being explained through a series of eye twitches and lip purses.

"It is sufficient that they step aside without causing bloodshed," Matilda responded. "Whether they remain in a new Gem society or go off on their own makes no difference to us, as long as they give up controlling the lives of the rest of the sisters, and don't oppose our attempts to restore biological diversity."

"Do you think they'll agree to that?" Kelly asked. This the senior clone understood without translation.

"No, but we believe it's important to ask," Matilda answered. "As the Free Gem spend more time around the other species, we have learned that there are many ways to make a revolution, and the most important part is to control the media. Our sisters who fled to worlds of some of the advanced species believe that in a short while, we will be able to force our message into the Empire with such power that Gem Today will not be able to compete."

"Are you sure you should be telling me this?" Kelly asked. "I'm not a revolutionary strategist, but if you do want to speak with an experienced human campaign planner, I'm sure I can arrange it."

Mist translated through another series of silent expressions and twitches, though this time she threw in a hand movement that looked to Kelly like she was drawing a sword and creating a knight.

"Yes, we would like to meet with a human warrior prince," Matilda replied. Kelly figured that was a reasonable enough description for Woojin, and it occurred to her that real royalty would probably call a council of war.

"I'd like to suggest that my staff and I create a workshop on negotiation for you to attend," Kelly suggested. "It was my best subject in diplomacy school, and I'm sure our, uh, warrior prince would agree that force is the last resort."

Mist translated again, this time engaging in an ever-broader array of pantomime, though Kelly couldn't imagine what was so difficult about her proposal.

"Are you going to teach us the ambassador game?" Sue asked.

Kelly cringed. Was there anybody in the galaxy who hadn't heard of her difficulties on Parents Day?

"That was just for children," she explained hastily. "There is quite a lot to negotiating, and role playing is just one of the exercises we'll use, though it's an important one."

"Playing with food?" Dorothy interrupted, after Mist nudged her for help.

"Not that kind of roll," Kelly explained. At times she wished that English wasn't so loaded with homonyms. "A role is when you pretend to be somebody, like when you and Mist take turns playing the role of Prince Phillip."

Mist nodded gravely and launched into a new series of silent explanations for the Free Gem delegation. She even had Dorothy bring the picture book, and seemed to be pointing out highlights of the plot to the older clones, whose intense attention to the performance was almost painful to watch. After waiting patiently for several minutes and finishing her tea, Kelly felt it was time to move the meeting back onto a grown-up basis.

"I don't want to spoil the workshop before you attend, but it would be helpful if we talked about what you should expect, so you can communicate with the rest of the Free Gem leadership to avoid confusion," Kelly interrupted gently.

Mist spun around, looking guilty, and asked Kelly to repeat herself. Dorothy was annoyed, because she thought she was beginning to crack the code of the silent conversation employed by the clones. Kelly was worried her daughter would develop a facial tic if she kept up her attempt to mimic her friend's expressions.

"I was just saying that your older sisters will get more out of the workshop if they prepare first," Kelly said.

Either Matilda was able to understand Kelly's words directly or Mist had managed the translation in record time, because the oldest clone replied almost immediately.

"Yes, please," Matilda said. "Tell us how to prepare." Then, to Kelly's surprise, the clone gave her a wink.

"Well, you start by setting goals, and also alternatives that you could live with," Kelly said uncertainly, confused by the clone's playful attitude. "You need to analyze, to, uh, think strongly about what the Empire Gem will want from the negotiation, and practice listening to what Ambassador Gem may say, even if it makes you angry. Emotional control is very important."

"Wait for her, Mommy, you're going too fast," Dorothy said, watching her friend in concern. But the expression on Mist's face that worried Dorothy was apparently just her interpretation of 'emotional control', and the young clone looked expectantly for the EarthCent ambassador to start again.

"We, uh, stress verbal communication, though I guess that won't be necessary in your case," Kelly continued. "But we do need to focus on problem solving, so you don't lose hope over some minor points of dispute that have little impact on your overall goal. I suppose you don't need practice at teamwork or coming to a consensus amongst yourselves, so we'll drop those exercises."

"What's a consensus?" Mist asked Dorothy, who shrugged her shoulders.

"An agreement amongst yourselves," Kelly explained.

"Yes, that's correct," Matilda replied, translating the short sentence herself. "I think we're all in agreement on how to move forward now."

Kelly wasn't sure why that sounded so ominous.

Nineteen

"I really thought we had a good chance at knife throwing," Shaina groused to Paul, as the Carnival committee members moved on to the next event venue. "Emile never missed a stationary target in our tryouts, and he was even spearing the balls I tossed into the air. The Carnival prospectus really should have made it clear that the contest included knife throwing AND catching. I thought the poor guy was going to have a heart attack."

"He was a heck of a good sport to stand in there and make a few grabs," Paul replied. "He told me afterwards he'd never had knives thrown at him before. Anyway, it's hard to see how anybody could beat the Dollnicks with their extra arms and long reach. What's next on the schedule?"

"Dancing," Brinda replied after glancing at her tab. "Hopefully it will be a little fairer than the Vergallian ballroom version."

"I think that Jingjing has a real shot at winning," Aisha said enthusiastically. "She was professionally trained in Chinese opera from childhood, and she acted in a number of immersives when she was younger. She even has a new performance piece ready to debut that represents the lifecycle of a tulip."

"I'd hold onto your betting money until the lead judge reads the rules," Stanley cautioned her. "Maybe it's traditional for the dancers to catch knives."

The lift tube opened and the humans spilled out into the lobby of the Drithalia Memorial Culture Center. The facility was located on one of the Verlock decks, and everybody quickly installed their nose filters. The air was hotter and drier than most of the station's biologicals would prefer, but it was within the permissible range for multi-species events.

"Is Kelly judging on this panel?" Shaina asked.

"She didn't feel qualified," Aisha replied.

"What does qualification have to do with it?" Ian demanded. "All she has to do is show up, and as Carnival Queen, her vote is worth as much as two other judges. That's a big deal on a five-judge panel."

"Easy, Ian," the senior Hadad said, reaching up to pat the pub owner's shoulder. "You should know by now that our ambassador isn't a cut-throat competitor."

"She's a milksop," Ian grumbled.

"Our seats are this way," Shaina called, cutting through an unoccupied row in the stone amphitheatre. "It must have cost the Verlocks a fortune to construct this place. Wow, the stone benches are even heated!"

The humans took their places just as the five judges filed in from an opening that must have led to a ready-room below the stage. Aisha recognized Bork and Czeros, but the other three ambassadors were all strangers to her, and she didn't even recognize the species of the judge with the gorgeous feathers.

"Does anybody know what the alien next to the bunny is?" she whispered.

"They're called K'dink, or K'plink, I'm not quite sure," Brinda whispered back. "I didn't think they were nitrogen/oxygen breathers, but maybe the ambassador is just holding his breath."

"How do you know it's a he?" her father asked.

"The males are the colorful ones," she replied. "The females are a bit drab."

The Grenouthian ambassador, who wore a golden sash of office, rose to his feet and began to speak.

"As the chairman of this Carnival's dance competition, I am required to go over the rules before we begin," the giant bunny proclaimed. "First and foremost, there will be no biting, gouging or joint manipulation. Use of paralytic strikes, even if the contact is judged to be incidental, will result in immediate disqualification."

"This doesn't sound promising," Stanley muttered to Aisha.

"Contestants will be judged on their individual expression through movement, in addition to the number of times they count coup on the other dancers," the Grenouthian continued. "As in all formal dance competitions, anybody moving beyond the rope circle, whether accidentally or thrown, will be immediately disqualified."

"She's going to get killed!" Aisha wailed. "And I'm the one who chose her over the Cossack guy with the jump dancing act. At least he would have been wearing boots!"

"Don't worry," Ian reassured her. "She looked like a tough cookie. Well, a small tough cookie."

A bell sounded, and the contestants emerged from multiple entrances onto the stage. Some of the dancers were armed with deadly-looking weapons, primarily swords and axes, though there was a Horten whirling five metal balls on narrow chains above his head. Jingjing was

197

dressed in a shapeless garment of brown silk, which with her arms held out in a hoop shape before her, made her look a little like a bulb.

"It's a free-for-all, Jingjing," Aisha yelled in the silence before the dance competition began. "Get out of there!"

A second bell sounded, and the packed aliens, over a hundred of them, began to dance about. Amazingly, no giant gouts of blood or detached limbs appeared flying through the air, and it quickly became apparent that the dancers weren't trying to maim each other as much as they were struggling to clear a space where they could perform. The humans lost sight of Jingjing, who wasn't a tall woman to begin with, and Aisha could only hope that she hadn't been crushed beneath the feet of the leaping mass of aliens.

"Is that one for real or some kind of simulation?" Ian asked, poking Stanley in the ribs with an elbow.

"I don't think I've ever seen a Vergallian woman dancing solo before," Donna's husband replied. He didn't have to ask who Ian was referring to, and most of the eyes on their side of the arena were on the perfect humanoid female, whose movements were hypnotically erotic in a non-species-specific sort of way.

"Don't look, Pop," Brinda said, covering her father's eyes with a hand. He pulled it down and held onto it, but Shaina covered her father's eyes from the other side, and then he ran out of hands.

"It's the Vergallian seduction dance," Shaina urgently addressed Stanley and Ian. "You guys better look away or you could end up following her out of here like a couple of lost puppies."

Just then, a sort of bubble of activity swelled up in the central mass of dancers, and many of them stumbled outwards in a domino effect. An enormous bunny backed into the Vergallian dancer, causing her to momentarily lose her balance and step over the rope. The attempt of those dancers at the expanding edge to retain their balance led to a push back in the direction of the center, and more contestants were forced over the rope at the opposite side of the circle, setting off another reaction. In less than a minute, more than half of the dancers had been disqualified, and many of those who remained were nursing accidental injuries from the scrum.

"So far so good," commented a Grenouthian fan seated in front of the humans. "Now we'll see some real dancing."

Sure enough, with ample space cleared for the remaining dancers to maneuver freely, the contest was transformed from a late-night brawl at a dance club into a more artistic event. The human tulip bulb germinated, reached for the sun, and burst into bloom. Then a Verlock flame dancer scorched one of her petals and she kicked him in the head.

"Intentional paralytic contact!" boomed a Verlock from the host's booster section on the other side of the arena.

"He attacked her costume," Ian yelled back.

The Grenouthian judge consulted with his colleagues and threw penalty flags at both dancers. Jingjing wilted gracefully, then she accepted her fate and followed the Verlock off the stage.

"That was unfair," Brinda objected. "We should lodge a protest."

"The judges are the ultimate authority for each contest, that much of the rules I understood," her father replied. "I'll give Jingjing credit, though, that was quite a kick. Must be the Chinese opera training."

The humans didn't stay for the rest of the dance competition, which was rapidly being reduced to a five-way contest between the dancers who were represented by a judge on the panel.

"What's next?" Ian asked, as they exited to the corridor.

"The only live competition left today is four-dimensional art," Brinda replied. "Cooking is in the tasting phase by now, and I've seen enough projectile vomiting brought on by cross-species cuisine to give it a pass. The two-dimensional and three-dimensional art contests are just static installations, no different than going to a gallery, so we can stop in any time."

"What is four-dimensional art, exactly?" Stanley asked. "I know we gave our slot to Dring because there weren't any human contenders, but I didn't get a chance to ask him what's involved."

"I think it has to do with creating a sculpture that expresses motion in a timed trial," Aisha replied. "I know that Dring does a lot of metal constructs, and he can work pretty quickly when he wants to, so maybe he'll have a chance."

"Will the ambassador be coming?" Ian asked. "I'm sure the rest of you have noticed by now that having a friendly judge on the panel is half the battle."

"She said she would come, but I don't know if she intends to judge or not," Aisha replied. "All of this nepotism and speciesism, it just doesn't seem to fit the spirit of Carnival."

"First of all, if speciesism is really a word, it shouldn't be," Ian retorted. "Second of all, what do you know about the spirit of Carnival? All of the aliens on the station except for the Chert have competed in plenty of Carnivals, and the Chert have at least watched them from the shadows.

200

We're probably the ones everybody is pointing at, saying that the humans are bad sports."

"Four-dimensional art contest," Shaina intoned, after the humans again crowded into a single lift tube capsule. When the doors slid open, they found themselves in a cavernous hold on the core. There were a few ships undergoing maintenance in the distance, but the real action was taking place behind a temporary wall of curtains, from beyond which bright flashes of welding lit up the surroundings.

"Wow, I've never been in a full maintenance bay before," Aisha commented. "The deck curvature is the same as Mac's Bones, but it seems to go on forever."

"Everybody take safety goggles," Stanley commanded, as they approached the end of the curtain wall. A series of bins with labels showing the compatibility for various species formed a blockade to remind vulnerable biologicals not to enter the area without eye protection. The humans fished out a variety of goggles and full-face protectors, and then took turns peeking around the edge of the curtains to make sure that the filters actuated properly.

"It looks more like a shipyard than an art competition," Ian observed, as they headed towards the hissing, sputtering and flashing arcs and flames. "Doesn't anybody work in stone anymore?"

"Probably takes too long," the Hadad patriarch replied. "Creepers! What's that thing?"

The humans gaped at the nightmarish sculpture of some sort of prehistoric Dollnick-eating insect that the towering Dolly was rapidly welding together out of rod stock, all four of his arms in continuous motion. If the pieces were to be judged on emotional content, it would be hard to beat this one for fear.

The next artist was moving ponderously back and forth between a giant cauldron and a dully glowing mass that bore a vague resemblance to a spacecraft.

"That Verlock is working with stone," Shaina pointed out to Ian. "At least, I guess it will be stone when it cools."

"Is he squeezing that lava out with just his hands?" her sister asked.

"No, he's using a piping bag," their father answered. "I'll have to check the temperature rating of the ones we're selling in Kitchen Kitsch. A molten-rock and fire rated bag for squeezing out frosting might make a good novelty item for chefs."

The humans continued moving through the area with the circulating crowd, keeping a safe distance from the artists and marveling over the technical competence on display. Some pieces were aesthetically pleasing through their symmetry or use of different colored construction materials, but none of them impressed the humans like the Dollnick nightmare.

"Hey!" called a helmeted figure, waving a hand. When he flipped up his visor, the human Carnival committee members all recognized Joe, who had brought his own welding helmet. Kelly moved out from behind him, holding a dark shield on a stick like an opera mask. Both were dressed in practical fireproof overalls from Mac's Bones.

"Are you judging?" Ian asked Kelly, dispensing with small talk.

"I don't know," she replied, sounding miserable. "If I do vote, Dring already made it clear that he'll expect my support, and that's not fair to anybody either."

"You and your daughter-in-law are the only sentients on the station who think that way," Ian scolded her. "Do you know what that means when it's a hundred million against two? It means that you're both crazy!"

"Have you found Dring yet?" Aisha asked the McAllisters, hoping to diffuse the confrontational atmosphere.

"We were just pointed in his direction by a trio of Fillinducks who were packing up their tools," Joe replied. "They said they knew when they were beat."

Forming a little clump of humanity, the committee members and the McAllisters followed Joe in the direction that the Fillinducks had indicated, and ended up on the fringes of a large crowd gathered around a sputtering light source. The flashes were visible off of the high ceiling doors of the bay, and the sounds of Dring's welding became audible as the noises produced by the remaining contestants began to fade out.

As the humans looked for an opening, they were surprised to see that some of the taller aliens who could watch Dring working were beginning to weep, groan, or wave their moveable parts, expressing grief and distress in a hundred alien ways. Kelly was dying of curiosity when she finally found a vantage point on top of a metal stairway, which she later found out was a Drazen artwork that had been abandoned mid-construction.

Dring's piece evoked universal memories of childhood trauma, of the tyranny of the strong over the weak, of the loss of innocence. It spoke to the common mythology of all sentients, the yearning to be free, the horror of being caged. The impression was somehow concrete and abstract at the same time, and gave Kelly the distinct feeling of being a bird with clipped wings.

As word spread, the other four-dimensional artists paused on construction of their own works to gather

203

around and watch Dring put the finishing touches on his masterpiece. The light metal sculpture somehow expressed such a weightiness that it was a wonder to all present that it didn't fall through deck after deck until exiting to the vacuum of space at the station's outer skin. The judges, when they were able to catch their collective breaths, unanimously awarded Dring the first prize without their usual posturing and bickering, saving Kelly from the need to make up her mind.

"Does your piece have a name?" Ambassador Crute asked Dring respectfully.

"Metoo unjustly grounded for helping his human friend," Dring recited in a voice that expressed the utter exhaustion of spent creative forces, colored with the satisfaction of a job well done.

The crowd applauded, and a couple of towering Dollnicks insisted on raising the little dinosaur onto their shoulders. A crew from the Grenouthian galactic news service captured it all with immersive equipment.

"It was just two days," Libby complained through Kelly's implant. "Besides, it was Firth's suggestion, and Metoo agreed that it was an important lesson."

Knowing how Dorothy could turn being sent to bed without dessert into a tragedy to rival the ancient Greeks, Kelly sympathized with the Stryx.

Twenty

The EarthCent embassy office wasn't large enough to host the meeting Kelly had called to get the other ambassadors caught up on the Gem situation. In order to thank Ian for his work on the Carnival committee and to console him for losing at his national sport, Donna scheduled the meeting at Pub Haggis in the Little Apple. Aisha went on ahead to discuss the menu details with the Ainsleys, and by the time that Kelly arrived with Samuel, Ian and Torra had laid out a full spread of food, none of which appeared to be Scottish.

Czeros was the first ambassador to arrive, quickly followed by Apria and Crute. Since all three represented species who had won a Carnival event, caber toss, ballroom dancing and knife throwing respectively, Kelly immediately assumed they arrived early for the sake of extra time to gloat. She was correct.

"Our man was very impressed that a human could be so competitive at ancestor worship," Czeros started in on Ian immediately. Behind the bar, Torra got her bagpipes off the shelf and began looking for her earplugs.

"Please, Czeros. As a personal favor, let's not talk about the caber toss competition," Kelly whispered to the Frunge ambassador, as Ian's ears turned red. "The poor man left his stick behind in Mac's Bones, he was so disappointed."

"Besides," Apria commented, stretching like a cat preparing for a big night out, "I doubt his wife would have approved of the prize I gave the winner."

"I'd rather talk about knife throwing in any case," Crute said. "Now there's a sport we can all enjoy."

Ortha arrived next, glared the other ambassadors into silence, and started eating without waiting for an invitation. He'd been getting a hard time both at home and at work for ruining his son's chances of winning hide-and-seek, and his patience was exhausted. Ortha's attack on the food proved a wise strategy for putting the taunting on temporary hold, because the other ambassadors were too experienced to waste their time talking while the best bits disappeared into the Horten's stomach.

Bork showed up next, able to hold his head high thanks to the Drazen victory in singing, a competition they won more often than not. When he saw that the other ambassadors were already eating, he threw Kelly a hurt look, and then hurried to get his share. The Grenouthian and Verlock ambassadors followed soon after. Now that the other members of the ad-hoc group were all in place, the Chert materialized right in front of the fruit bowl and started snatching at toothpicks to transfer some choice bits to his plate.

"Thank you all for coming on short notice," Kelly announced over the sounds of alien ingestion and mastication. "I think the recent developments with the Gem Empire and the Free Gem movement lend a sense of urgency to our meeting. Also, the local dissidents asked me to arrange for negotiations with Ambassador Gem on this station."

"I was about to request a new meeting myself," the Verlock ambassador droned slowly, tapping the table. At first Kelly was relieved that somebody was paying attention, but then she remembered that the Verlocks didn't find human food palatable, though their digestive systems were Drazen-like in their robustness. "As a species which shares a number of star systems with the Gem Empire, we have seen a large and sudden increase in the number of Gem seeking transit through our space stations and tunnel connections."

"Did the surge begin with the broadcast of Gem Tomorrow?" Kelly asked.

"Exactly," the Verlock replied. "Our intelligence analysts now believe that the majority of the Gem wish to see the end of the current Empire, a view that was unimaginable to us just a cycle ago."

"Why isn't that one eating?" Ian muttered in an aside to Aisha. Despite his recent humiliation at the hands of the aliens, the Scotsman was first and foremost a victualler, and it bothered him to see a guest ignoring the food.

"The Verlocks don't like watery or sweet food," Aisha told him. "Don't worry about it. Kelly said he never eats at these meetings."

"Did everybody receive a syllabus for the negotiation workshop EarthCent will be hosting in my home for the Free Gem delegation?" Kelly asked. She received a few skeptical looks in return, and Apria loudly spit out a seed. Surprisingly, the Grenouthian ambassador pushed his plate away and cleared his furry throat.

"I showed your treatment to some local producers of children's entertainment," the giant bunny replied. "They would like to meet with you to discuss creating a humorous immersive for pre-school edutainment. And before any of our esteemed colleagues spill the beans, I want to disclose that I will receive a finder's fee if your script is adapted, but I assure you I was motivated by my love for children, not the money."

Kelly turned bright red and bit her tongue. She and Aisha had worked for hours on the workshop outline, recalling all of their favorite exercises from EarthCent's diplomatic training course.

"Excellent skin color," Ortha complimented her between bites. "How very Horten of you."

"I know that all of the so-called advanced species take negotiation skills for granted, but that didn't stop our man from winning the bartering competition, now did it!" Kelly retorted, her jaw jutting out.

The ambassadors fell uncharacteristically silent, even pausing in their demolition of the finger food. For the humans to win one of the permanent Carnival events in their first outing was considered a major upset. When Mr. Clavitts had not only walked away with the bartering prize but had done so in record time, the aliens couldn't help being impressed.

"Perhaps if you included that man in your workshop plan?" Crute suggested.

"The Gem have no tradition of bartering or negotiation in their culture," Kelly continued with renewed confidence. "This also applies to their ambassadors, whose traditional role on the Stryx stations has been to complain about how all the other species envy them. We, Aisha and I, believe that with the proper preparation, our local Free Gem have a good chance of changing the course of the Empire without resorting to force."

"How very human," Ortha muttered darkly.

"Let us accept, for the sake of argument, that our absent colleague Ambassador Gem has both the authority and the bad sense to conclude a deal that would result in her immediate dismissal," the Vergallian ambassador posited sweetly. Kelly flinched, since she knew from experience that Apria only smiled when she was about to sink in her claws. "That would make the proposed negotiations the most important event for Gem civilization in tens of thousands of years. Why, if everything goes as you intend, the rest of us may even stop thinking of them as nasty clones."

"What's your point, Apria?" Bork grunted, coming to Kelly's defense.

"I just want to lend my support for her workshop idea," Apria replied innocently. "Perhaps the best possible use of our time today would be to ask the ambassador and her assistant to stage the workshop for us here, so we can offer a helpful critique."

"I suppose that might be useful," Kelly said cautiously. "But there's only the two of us to act at least three parts, and I think it would make the most sense if I played myself."

"I shall be honored to accept the role of Ambassador Gem," Apria said graciously. "And perhaps your sidekick will take the part of a Free Gem negotiator?"

"It won't work." Aisha spoke directly to the Vergallian ambassador, surprising Kelly with her assertiveness. "Our plan is tailored to the fact that the Gem share a form of clone empathy or partial telepathy, which you'd know if you had reviewed the materials. There's no point in acting out the scenarios when you and I have no clue what one another is thinking or feeling."

"I stand corrected," Apria said coldly. "Perhaps you could summarize the important points of your workshop for one so ignorant as myself."

"Ambassadors, please," the Verlock protested. "Our analysts predict that in the absence of political change, the better part of forty billion clones will eventually be seeking new homes. The Gem fleeing the Empire will avoid Verlock worlds due to environmental incompatibility, but I assure you that they will soon be arriving at your doors in large numbers."

"We are seeing some of that already," Ortha admitted. "And having read through the human materials myself, I'm afraid I must concur with the Grenouthians. Despite a certain charming naivety, I don't see how the workshop exercises can help the clones reach a compromise. The basic assumption seems to be that both parties are rational actors, where we all know that it's rare for diplomatic negotiations to include even one rational actor."

"You make it sound like we're on a hopeless mission," Kelly complained. "As my colleague has already pointed out, if the Gem can't resolve this issue through reform, it's likely that the Empire will produce a wave of refugees like the galaxy hasn't seen since..."

"Since last Carnival?" the Chert interrupted, having finished off all of the fresh cantaloupe and honeydew melon grown locally on the human ag deck. "I understand your concern, Ambassador, but the galaxy sees a constant flux of refugees. Before my people found a new home and joined the tunnel network, we were refugees for more than a hundred thousand years. The Gem are already part of the network so the Stryx will help them."

"That's your plan?" Kelly asked, staring at the other ambassadors. "Why even get together to meet if we're going to count on the Stryx to do all of the heavy lifting?"

"They do anyway," Bork reminded her gently.

"But isn't it important that we try?" Kelly exclaimed. "I know that you've all been around a lot longer than humans and you've seen species come and go, but this involves us personally. I think of the Free Gem as my friends."

"Do you think we're just here for the food and wine?" Czeros said, even though there wasn't any wine on the table. Aisha took the hint and whispered to Torra, who pulled a bottle from the rack and gave it to the acting junior counsel. The Ainsleys had actually been good sports about Ian's loss, but neither of them were quite ready to wait on the Frunge, especially after his earlier comment.

"Well, maybe," Kelly answered him uncertainly. "I thought our last meeting was productive, so I guess the problem must be me."

"Nonsense," Czeros replied, cheered by the sight of Aisha removing the cork from a bottle of red. "It's just that some of the present company don't understand your objection to Stryx help when you are, after all, the only foster species present, not to mention your recent election victory."

"Your choice not to vote on any of the judging panels was discussed at the Naturals League post-Carnival party," Bork added. "Most of the species thought that you were trying to show up their ancestors by violating a tradition that extends back for thousands of Carnivals, but I assured them that it was just a quirk of your personality."

Kelly gratefully accepted an unexpected glass of wine from Czeros and then took a moment to absorb the criticisms of the other ambassadors. She replayed the comments in her head to "hear" them, a technique she intended to explain to the Gem in the workshop.

During the conversational lull, Ian came forward with a small wooden box and offered it to the Verlock ambassador. Srythlan sniffed at the contents, and then tried a piece of whatever it was. After a bite, the bulky alien bowed his head at the pub owner, who smiled in satisfaction that none of his guests would go away hungry.

"So do you think that our workshop idea is just a quirk of my personality as well?" Kelly finally asked her friend.

"We're all sure you have excellent reasons to publicly promote negotiations," he replied, which struck the EarthCent ambassador as a strange response to come from a diplomat. "It's hard to imagine Ambassador Gem will agree to any concessions, but nobody can fault you for trying. It seems to me that there was a civilization somewhere, once, that averted civil war through negotiations."

"I think I heard that too," Czeros said in support of his traditional rival, while casting an appreciative look around the well-provisioned table.

"Yes, the, er, uh," Crute stammered.

"Maybe. Once," Apria agreed sourly.

"You see?" Bork said. "Perhaps your workshop will enable your friends to convince Ambassador Gem that everything she believes is wrong, and she'll be the first of the Gem elite to step down. Stranger things have happened."

"Uh, thanks, Bork," Kelly said, wishing she could believe that the ambassadors were suddenly being nice because they appreciated her professionalism, rather than the catering.

"We should consider a fallback position, just in case the ambassador's plan somehow falls short," the Verlock ambassador added diplomatically, tapping on the table with one of the hard, white biscuits to force his speech into a faster rhythm.

"Let's look at the options," the Grenouthian said, pausing from his self-assigned task of wrapping various food items in napkins to bring home. "The worst case is, what? That the Empire continues to exist and a huge number of low-skill clones flood the tunnel network worlds, while enough Gem remain loyal to retain their current real estate."

"That would be destabilizing," Apria agreed.

"We might offer them transport to a habitable world, rather than trying to absorb them," Crute suggested. "Perhaps the former home system of the Brupt?"

"Those planets aren't exactly in ready-to-occupy condition," Kelly objected, remembering the virtual shopping trip Libby had given the EarthCent staff for potential Kasilian homes.

"I wasn't finished yet," the Grenouthian complained. "That was just the worst-case scenario, not the most likely. Another possibility is that the recent outflows represent those Gem most likely to leave, and the Empire may stabilize. Our analysts don't agree with the Verlock assessment on this point. Or, the Free Gem might take over, and we could get a wave of refugees from the former elites who are unfit for any work."

"Assuming we aren't going to offer military assistance to either side, I think that lining up a potential world or two for whoever ends up homeless may be the cheapest solution for us all in the end," Czeros said.

"The Stryx always keep a few nice worlds hidden for biological emergencies," the Chert ambassador offered, then looked embarrassed.

"None of us are in a position to offer up a planet in any condition on our own authority," Bork said. "Why don't we each talk the situation over with our people and plan on meeting again when the situation warrants a response."

"Good idea, Bork," the Vergallian ambassador said. "I am supposed to be appearing at a celebration for our victorious dance team as we speak, so thank you for the food, and I'll be on my way."

As usual, the moment one ambassador made a break for the door, the rest vanished as quickly as they could stuff their pockets with leftovers and mumble an excuse. Czeros remained behind because there was still a glass of wine left in the bottle, and Bork stayed to be sociable.

Just before the Grenouthian exited the pub, he turned around and called back to Kelly, "The offer for the workshop show still stands. I don't think that my producers would have any problem with dual use."

"What were those biscuits you gave the Verlock?" Kelly asked Ian, pointedly ignoring the Grenouthian. "I've never seen him actually eat cross-species before."

"Biscuits?" Ian gave her a strange look. "That was salt cod. And from the way he took to it, I think we may have discovered a new market."

"Do you think the Grenouthian was just being sarcastic about wanting to develop our workshop into a children's show?" Aisha asked.

"Don't take it personally, Aisha," Kelly told her daughter-in-law. "They're always making fun of humans for one thing or another. The Grenouthians ran out of original entertainment ideas ages ago. That's why they mainly produce documentaries."

"I wasn't offended," Aisha protested. "I was thinking that I don't know if I'm cut out for diplomacy in the long run. Maybe I'd do better working with children."

"I know they pay well," Bork contributed. "I do a little acting in historical dramas as a hobby, you know, and I'm always hearing that the Grenouthians pay top cred when it comes to working in the immersives."

"Et tu, Bork?" Kelly exclaimed soulfully.

"Never attempt to win by force what can be won by deception," the Drazen ambassador countered.

"Hey, that's from Machiavelli," Kelly said in surprise.

"Who?" Aisha asked.

"I rest my case," Bork said with a flourish. "At least consider the Grenouthian offer. As my father always told me, you can lead an acting junior consul to water, but you can't make her swim."

Twenty-One

Joe was putting a new group of EarthCent Intelligence trainees through their paces when a strange scrabbling sound, followed by a loud clatter, started coming from the direction of the converted ice harvester. He backpedalled a few steps away from the column of joggers for a clear line of sight, and saw that a few pieces of patio furniture had been knocked over. But there weren't any children sprawled on the ground, and now that he thought about it, he had seen Dorothy and Mist heading over to Dring's a few minutes earlier.

Before he could tell the recruits to take a break while he went to investigate, the crazed scrabbling noise repeated, this time coming from the other side of the column of trainees. Joe tensed as a gap suddenly opened in their line, with several of the joggers collapsing to the deck as an enormous black shape bowled through them. Warnings were shouted as the scrabbling started up again and the beast launched itself towards their drillmaster.

"Down, boy!" Joe shouted to no avail, as the excited puppy once again forgot about the lack of cornering traction to be had on the metal deck. Claws scratched frantically, but the dog only managed to turn itself broadside to the owner of Mac's Bones, before slamming into his legs like a giant furry cannonball. The two went down in a heap, and the recruits looked on in amazement as the giant beast began to lick their trainer's face. Joe tried to fend off the attack and to get a closer look at the dog at the same time, which wasn't easy to do with his eyes squinched shut against a giant, wet tongue.

"Beowulf?" he asked.

On hearing his name, the puppy sat back on his haunches and tried to look innocent. With paws the size of dinner plates, it was clear that the pure-bred Huravian hound would be even larger than the original Beowulf when he filled out.

"Uh, five-minute break," Joe instructed the gaping recruits. "No, better yet, do a lap around the hold while I take care of this."

The future intelligence agents shuffled off in an uninspired jog, a few of them nursing limps from their unexpected service as a puppy backstop. Joe regarded the reincarnation of his old friend, trying to figure out how much of the old Beowulf was still there. It hadn't yet occurred to Joe to wonder how the dog had suddenly showed up at Mac's Bones, when he heard a hail from the direction of the entrance.

"Sorry, Joe," Laurel called, wiping the tears of laughter from her eyes. "We couldn't hold him back, but it was so funny!"

"Laurel! Patches!" Joe strode over to greet them, keeping a grip on Beowulf's ruff. "How did you find him?"

"He found us," Paul's former co-pilot from the Raider/Trader squadron explained. "We swapped duty with a chef and purser's assistant on the Union Station run to bring him home as quickly as possible. We thought it would be better to make it a surprise, just in case we were wrong about recognizing the incarnation."

"Were you on a Huravian route?" Joe asked. "I didn't think they were social enough to attract the cruise lines. We'd been thinking about taking a family vacation out that way ourselves, just to check in with the monks who breed the war dogs. I've been studying up on the whole thing, and supposedly they set aside the puppies that show signs of remembering a previous life."

"Beowulf latched onto me two weeks ago when we stopped at Hearth Station, and he wasn't going to let us go anywhere without him," Laurel explained. "We don't know where he came from before that, but I asked the Stryx librarian, and it seems he had been patrolling the arrivals area for a month, sniffing humans and mooching meals. We had to put him in stasis for the trip, though. Cruise line wouldn't accept a loose animal his size without proof of toilet training."

"Here, I saved his begging bowl," Patches added, handing Joe a large plastic bowl emblazoned with an image of a dog looking up at the stars. "According to the Hearth Station librarian, when the Huravian monks are convinced that a puppy really is a reincarnation, they give it the special bowl and somebody escorts it to one of the stations."

"It's funny, but after Beowulf found me, Patches and I both realized that we'd seen plenty of Huravian reincarnations hanging about the main transit points on the tunnel network, trying to pick up a familiar scent," Laurel said. "I've fed enough of them without even thinking about it. I guess I always assumed they belonged to somebody who was trying to sort out a lost luggage claim."

"Dorothy is going to be so thrilled that I'm almost afraid to see it," Joe said, still maintaining his grip on the dog. "What do you think, boy? Can you meet Dorothy without knocking her down?"

Beowulf shook his head up and down rapidly and gave a little whine of impatience. He had calmed down enough to begin paying attention to the scents assailing his nose, and he was eager to be on the trail.

"Alright," Joe said, releasing his hold. "Just wait—Hey!"

For a moment, the puppy looked like he was running in place on ice, his claws scratching at the metal flooring. Then he gained enough forward momentum that his paws started to find traction, and he accelerated off towards the passage through the scrap heap.

"Slow down or you'll impale yourself on something, you crazy mutt!" Joe yelled after him.

Either Beowulf remembered from his former incarnation's mercenary days that impaling was bad, or he recognized that the metal scrap wouldn't be as forgiving a backstop as the bodies of humans, because he locked all four legs and slowly skidded to a halt, well before the improvised partition that separated Dring's parking spot from the rest of Mac's Bones. From there, he moved cautiously, placing one paw at a time, as if the deck had a crust he was afraid to break through. Then he disappeared into the passage.

"You two go see Kelly and the baby, she came home early for a meeting today," Joe told the young couple. "I'll be finished up here in a little while."

"Are you running some sort of day camp for adults?" Laurel asked, as the ragged line of recruits straggled in from their circuit of the hold.

"Sort of a training camp for EarthCent Intelligence agents," Joe explained. "Secrecy isn't our strong suit."

219

Laurel and Patches walked up the ramp of the ice harvester and knocked at the frame of the open hatch that served as a front door. Kelly said, "Come in," without looking up. She was arranging place settings on the big table and it looked like she was expecting a lot of guests.

"Hi, Kelly," Laurel said, hiding any disappointment she might have felt at the casual reception.

The ambassador's head jerked up at the voice and she turned to stare at the young couple.

"Laurel and Patches, what a surprise!" she cried, running forward to give each of them a hug. "You haven't seen our Samuel in almost a year, he'll be two before you know it. But he's asleep now, so don't wake him. Did you see Joe and Dorothy? She'll be so excited."

"She's probably all excited already, Mrs. McAllister," Patches said politely.

Kelly looked puzzled for a moment, but then she remembered that she was in the middle of preparing for the Gem negotiation workshop.

"I hope you plan to stay with us while you're on the station," Kelly said rapidly. "You've caught me in the middle of getting ready for a diplomacy workshop we're putting on for the Free Gem, to help them prepare for their negotiations with the Empire. They should be arriving any minute. You're welcome to stay and watch, of course."

"Watch?" Laurel replied with a smile. "You just relax and get ready, and Patches and I will handle the kitchen and the hospitality. We're professionals, don't forget."

"Aisha's already in there cooking," Kelly called after them as they headed into the kitchen, but the truth was, she could probably use the help, since all twelve of the Free Gem who made up the local leadership were invited.

"Ambassador?" Libby's voice spoke in her ear. "There's a broadcast of Gem Tomorrow beginning. I suggest you sit down and watch."

Kelly glanced out the door to see if the Free Gem delegation had reached Mac's Bones yet. There was no sign of them, which was strange, since the clones were usually early. A large hologram popped into view over the projector where Paul usually played Nova with Jeeves, so Kelly settled onto the couch to watch. A professional music track that reminded her of the Grenouthian news service was just winding down, and a well-dressed clone standing at a lectern appeared.

"Welcome to Gem Tomorrow," the clone began, her shallow breathing belying her calm demeanor. "We're broadcasting live from the studios of the former Gem Today with a message for our sisters all over the galaxy. The revolution has come, and we have won!"

The screen suddenly cut to a series of views showing clones wearing uniforms slumped over desks or the controls of ships, sprawled in hallways, and even collapsed outdoors. Teams of lower caste Gem were moving about with stretchers, picking up some bodies for removal, and even more strangely, administering an injection in the arms of others.

"What's happening, Libby?" Kelly asked. "Has there been a surprise attack? Are they all dead? Are my Gem alright?"

"Everything appears to be going according to plan," the Stryx librarian replied. "Just wait and listen."

After several minutes of the video montage, the scenes of which were plainly recorded from far-flung locations all around Gem space, the studio announcer reappeared.

"Less than an hour ago, our sisters put into motion a daring plan to bloodlessly overthrow the entrenched elites of the Empire," the announcer continued. "A suspended animation drug obtained from the Farlings was added to the nutrition drink supply for the high tables throughout the population centers of the Empire and the capital ships of the fleet. We all owe a debt of gratitude to our waitress sisters who carried out the secret plan, conceived by the human ambassador on Union Station."

"What are they talking about?" Kelly cried, bringing the kitchen crew running and waking the baby from his nap. "I didn't say anything about drugging half of the Empire into a coma. I recommended negotiations!"

"The Farling antidote is being administered to our working class sisters who were unavoidably dosed along with the elites," the Gem Tomorrow announcer continued. "The deposed leadership will remain unconscious for one or two cycles, allowing us ample time to establish a new government and prevent any attempts on their part to regain power. For the time being, they will be collected by maintenance crews and stored in dormitories, where they will be provided with intravenous fluids as necessary."

"You have a visitor," Libby announced brightly, killing the volume on the hologram. Everybody looked towards the open door as Gwendolyn entered. The clone's face displayed a strange mix of exultation and anxiety, and she clutched a gift bag from the Chocolate Emporium in front of her like a shield.

"Gwendolyn! What's happening?" Kelly demanded, trying to prevent hysteria from creeping into her voice. "Hold on, I'll find the translation box," she added.

"I have a translation implant now," Waitress Gem reassured her. "I'm the first one, so the other sisters sent me to talk to you. Some of them are worried that you'll be angry about our pretending to go ahead with negotiations, but I told them it was all part of your plan."

"Plan? What plan was that?" Kelly demanded, struggling to maintain control. "My plan was to engage the Empire Gem in meaningful discussions in order to reach a compromise and establish fair elections. You put them all to sleep!"

"But that was your plan," Gwendolyn insisted stubbornly. "We had to guess at what you meant in parts since you disguised it as a children's story. Matilda said you did that for the sake of plausible deniability as a neutral diplomat, but the whole business about the good fairies putting the whole kingdom to sleep until the prince could awaken the princess was pretty clear."

"But that's the plot from Sleeping Beauty!" Kelly protested. "I didn't tell you any of that."

The ambassador and the clone stared at each other in mutual disbelief. The spell was only broken when Dorothy and Mist charged into the room.

"Mommy! Mommy! Beowulf is back! Daddy is keeping him outside until he calms down again so he doesn't wreck the house," Dorothy cried in excitement. "Where's Laurel?"

But it was Mist who captured the attention of the ambassador and the Free Gem. The girl screeched to a halt when she saw Kelly and Gwendolyn looking at her suspiciously. At that moment, the hide-and-seek champion would have sold her soul for a Chert invisibility projector.

"Just one minute!" Kelly ordered, but Gwendolyn had already begun interrogating the girl, and the two clones stared at each other in the focused way the Gem had when they were communicating without speech. After a minute, the older clone turned towards Kelly with an apologetic smile.

"Mist admits that she was so excited from reading the picture book with your daughter that she got it all mixed up with what you were telling us about negotiations," Gwendolyn explained. "She says she meant to correct herself, but every time she tried, we all told her how proud we were of her English and didn't listen. And when the Stryx gave her the ten-million-cred gift coin for Farling Pharmaceuticals, we assumed you'd fixed it with them, like the Carnival election."

"Ten million creds for winning at hide-and-seek!" Kelly squeaked. "I think I recognize the lion by the print of its paw." She plucked Samuel out of his playpen, where he had been loudly protesting being awakened in a sudden manner, and handed the boy to Gwendolyn. Then she put her fists on her hips and asked the ceiling, "Is your Sleeping Beauty revolution really going well, Libby?"

"Smooth as the little bear's porridge or Rapunzel's golden hair," the station librarian replied.

"I guess this means your sisters won't be coming for my diplomacy workshop," Kelly said to Gwendolyn, trying not to sound too disappointed that her own plan had been displaced by something better. "I don't suppose there's any point in getting Gem Tomorrow to issue a retraction about my involvement, since nobody will believe it anyway."

"We just wanted to make sure they gave you full cred-it," the Free Gem representative said, and for just the second time Kelly could remember, the clone began to laugh. "Matilda spent hours searching for human quotes about war since you enjoy them so much," Gwendolyn continued when she caught her breath. "She came up with,

'All warfare is based on deception,' but I guess in this case, we all deceived ourselves."

A loud snarling came from outside, and everybody heard Joe shouting, "Leave it! Leave it!" The snarling continued and rose in volume, and as Kelly and the others followed Dorothy and Mist back down the ramp, she heard Joe say, "Fine. Do whatever the hell you want, but don't expect me to throw it for you."

Scratching at the floor in an attempt to back up, Beowulf had a death grip on the tapered end of Ian's caber, holding it up so that only the heavy butt end was contacting the deck. Paw by paw, he dragged it towards the ice harvester. After expending a great deal of energy and slobber, he dropped it at Joe's feet.

"Well, I guess that deserves a beer," Joe said grudgingly, scratching behind the massive puppy's ears.

"Are you kidding?" Kelly objected. "Even if Beowulf really is inside there, he's just a puppy now. No beer until he's at least, uh, three."

Beowulf looked at her in shock, cocking his giant head. Then he scratched the deck methodically with his right forepaw, three times.

"People years," Kelly pronounced the dread sentence. Beowulf gave a little whine, and then settled to the deck to gnaw on the caber for consolation.

"Well, look what the galaxy dragged in," Jeeves declared. He settled on the deck and rolled up to the dog, who sniffed at the Stryx suspiciously. "Congratulations on your revolution, Gwendolyn. Ambassador, this just came for you," Jeeves added, extending a present.

"Oh, look at the pretty wrapping," Dorothy said.

"Are you going to ask Metoo to open it for you?" Mist inquired.

"Let us do it, Mommy. We won't rip anything," Dorothy promised.

Kelly let her daughter take the package and was turning back to ask Jeeves how the Stryx could possibly square their noninterference claims with footing the bill for the Free Gem coup, when her implant chimed in with, "Call from mother."

"Mom?" Kelly subvoced. "It's a little crazy here right now. Is anything wrong?"

"Everybody is talking about your honorable mention on Gem Tomorrow," her mother told her immediately. "All of the Earth networks interrupted their regular programming to show the feed from the Grenouthian Galactic News. I already got solicited for a quote, so I told them you are very dedicated to your job and that I'm sure you have humanity's best interests at heart, whatever the commentators are saying."

"But I didn't do anything," Kelly objected. "It's all based on a big misunderstanding, and it's as much your fault as mine."

"Really, Kelly. Aren't you a bit old to be blaming things on your mother?"

"It was the storybook you sent for Dorothy," Kelly protested. "She and her little Gem friend read it over and over again, and when the girl tried translating diplomatic advice to her older sisters for me, she was so excited by the story that she mixed it in."

"It's been decades since I read the book myself, but I do seem to recall the older sisters being a big part of the problem," her mother observed. "I am glad to hear it arrived safely since I've never used the diplomatic bag service before. Anyway, I was just calling to let you know that you're famous, again, and to remind you that your father and I are coming to visit next month."

"I think they were fairies, not older sisters," Kelly corrected her mother reflexively. "And most of them were good."

"I'm quite sure they were evil, or at least, mean-spirited," her mother insisted. "Didn't they make her scrub the floors and clean the chimney while they went to the ball?"

"It's another princess story!" Dorothy cried excitedly, after carefully extracting the book from the wrapping paper with the help of Mist.

"Cin-der-ell-a," the young Gem read the title.

"I'm not talking about the new book, Mom," Kelly said. "You sent her Sleeping Beauty last month."

"Not me," her mother replied with concern. "When my daughter can't keep her books straight I know she's been working too hard. I've got to run now, somebody at the door. Probably another reporter."

Kelly wanted to pursue the gift argument, but the call had already disconnected. It was amazing how her mother's conversational habits had changed since she stopped calling collect and started footing the bill for the Stryx tunneling communications herself. Then it hit Kelly that she knew exactly what was happening.

"Jeeves!" Kelly practically screamed, but the Stryx was nowhere to be seen.

"Jeeves go bye-bye," Samuel observed happily from Gwendolyn's arms.

"Joe! Sammy just said his first real sentence!" Kelly exclaimed, momentarily forgetting her anger.

"Uh, I think he said something about Libby to me the other day," Joe replied, and squinted one eye as he tried to remember. "Libby hide now?"

"His first sentence too?" Kelly wailed dramatically. "The Stryx have been getting into everything again. They even used a phony gift to Dorothy to manipulate the Gem into revolting!"

"What's a phony gift?" Joe asked. "Do you mean they brought her a present and then took it back?"

"No, they gave her an illustrated copy of Sleeping Beauty and tricked me into thinking it was from my Mom," Kelly groused. Somehow, it didn't sound so nefarious when she said it out loud. "Now the workshop Aisha and I spent weeks preparing for has been cancelled, and the girls are cooking up a storm with no guests."

Beowulf barked once to draw everybody's attention, and then he pulled in his stomach to make his already prominent ribcage stand out even more.

"I don't think using up the food will be a problem," Joe said with a laugh. "But you may as well ping a few people and we'll have a picnic. I'll invite Dring and Lynx. I think you told me Woojin was coming for the workshop. Just tell Donna to round up the usual suspects and I'll get the barbeque going in case somebody else wants meat for a change."

"Libby?" Kelly asked out loud. "Couldn't you figure out how to fix the galaxy once in a while without tricking me into something?"

"You know we don't believe in directly interfering with the progress of biologicals," Libby answered. "Now Gryph has something to ask if you have a minute."

Dorothy and Mist broke off from reading Cinderella to listen to the interesting grown-up conversation. It wasn't often Gryph said anything in the hearing of children.

"I know I haven't finished listening to all of the complaints yet. I'll get to it soon," Kelly pleaded.

"It's time to ask about your prize, Ambassador," Gryph said. "It's traditional to award the Carnival Queen with a gift after a successful celebration, so just make a wish. And we do appreciate your assistance with diffusing the Gem situation and helping to nudge them back towards a more promising future."

"She should get three wishes!" Dorothy interrupted.

"It's always three wishes," Mist confirmed, nodding in agreement.

"Does anybody take them all at once?" Gryph inquired.

"No," Dorothy replied slowly. "You usually need the second wish to fix the first wish, and the third wish to put the genie back in the bottle."

"One wish for now, then," Gryph continued. "What shall it be?"

"How many more complaints do I have to listen to?" Kelly asked.

"Just a hundred and seventy-one left," Gryph told her. "You could get through them in less than twenty hours."

"Can you make them all go away?" Kelly asked.

"If that's your wish," Gryph replied. "But you just lost me a bet with Jeeves. That's exactly what he predicted you'd do."

EarthCent Ambassador Series:

Date Night on Union Station

Alien Night on Union Station

High Priest on Union Station

Spy Night on Union Station

Carnival on Union Station

Wanderers on Union Station

Vacation on Union Station

Guest Night on Union Station

Word Night on Union Station

Party Night on Union Station

Review Night on Union Station

Family Night on Union Station

Book Night on Union Station

LARP Night on Union Station

About the Author

E. M. Foner lives in Northampton, MA with an imaginary German Shepherd who's been trained to bite bankers. The author welcomes reader comments at e_foner@yahoo.com.

You can sign up for new book announcements on the author's website - IfItBreaks.com

CPSIA information can be obtained
at www.ICGtesting.com
Printed in the USA
LVHW112332100123
736462LV00011B/304